SEAS

Chesterfield

LONDON

LITTLEHAMPTON

THE
GALAPAGOS
ISLANDS

DS'03

THE PIRATES!

In an Adventure with Scientists

THE PIRATES!

In an Adventure with Scientists

Gideon Defoe

Pantheon Books

NEW YORK

Library of Congress Cataloging-in-Publication Data
Defoe, Gideon.
The pirates! : in an adventure with scientists / Gideon Defoe.
p. cm.
ISBN 0-375-42321-4
I. Darwin, Charles, 1809–1882—Fiction.   2. *Beagle* (Ship)—Fiction.
3. Scientists—Fiction.   4. Pirates—Fiction.
I. Title: Pirates! in an adventure with scientists.   II. Title.
PR6104.E525P57 2004   823'.92—dc22   2004044570

Printed in the United States of America
First American Edition
4 6 8 9 7 5

To Sophie,
who has a quarter of a million pounds

CONTENTS

One

INTO ACTION UNDER THE PIRATE FLAG!

'The best bit about being a pirate,' said the pirate with gout, 'is the looting.'

'That's rubbish!' said the albino pirate. 'It's the doubloons. Doubloons are easily the best bit about pirating.'

The rest of the pirates, sunning themselves on the deck of the pirate boat, soon joined in. It had been several weeks since the Pirates' Adventure with Cowboys, and they had a lot of time on their hands.

'It's the pirate grog!'

'Marooning! That's what I like best!'

'Cutlasses!'

'The Spanish Main!'

'The ship's biscuits!'

One of the pirates pulled a special face to show exactly what he thought of this last comment, and soon all the pirates were fighting. With a sound like a bat hitting a watermelon, pirate fist connected with pirate jaw and a gold tooth bounced across the deck. The pirate with gout found himself run through in a grisly manner, and one of the cabin boys accidentally got a shiny pirate hook in the side of the head. It would probably have gone on for hours in this fashion, but both of the heavy wooden doors that led to the downstairs of the boat crashed open, and out onto the deck strode the Pirate Captain himself.

The Pirate Captain cut an impressive figure. If you were to compare him to a type of tree—and working out what sort of tree they would be if they were trees instead of pirates was easily one of the crew's favourite pastimes—he would undoubtedly be an oak, or maybe a horse chestnut. He was all teeth and curls, but with a pleasant, open face; his coat was of a better cut than everybody else's, and his beard was fantastic and glossy, and the ends of it were twisted with expensive-looking ribbons. Living at sea tended to leave you with ratty, matted hair, but the Pirate Captain somehow kept his beard silky and in good condition, and though nobody knew his secret, they all respected him for it. They also respected him because it was said he was wedded to the sea. A lot of pirates claimed that they were wedded to the sea, but usually this was an excuse because they couldn't get a girlfriend or they were gay pirates, but in the Pirate Captain's case none of his crew doubted he was actually wedded to the sea for a minute. Any of his men would have gladly taken a bullet for him, or even the pointy end of a cutlass. The Pirate Captain didn't need to do much more than clear his throat and roll his eyes a bit to stop the fighting dead in its tracks.

'What's going on, you scurvy knaves!' he bellowed. Pirates were often rude to each other, but without really meaning it, so none of the brawling pirates took being called a 'scurvy knave' too much to heart.

'We were just discussing what the best bit about being a pirate is,' answered the pirate dressed in green, after a bit of an awkward pause.

'The best bit about being a pirate?'

'Yes sir. We couldn't quite decide. I mean, it's all good . . .'

'The best bit about being a pirate is the shanties.'

And with the argument settled, the Pirate Captain strode back into the galley, indicating for the pirate with a scarf to follow. The rest of the crew were left on their own.

'He's right. It's the shanties,' said the albino pirate thoughtfully. One of the other pirates nodded.

'They *are* really good. Shall we sing a pirate shanty?'

The Pirate Captain was secretly relieved when he heard the strains of a rowdy shanty coming through the roof of the galley. Just recently he had been worrying about discipline on board the pirate boat, and there was an old pirate motto: If the men are singing a shanty, then they can't be up to mischief.*

'Come into my office for a moment,' he told the pirate with a scarf, who was his trusty second in command. The Pirate Captain's office was full of mementoes from the previous pirate adventures. There was a ten-gallon hat from the Pirates' Adventure with Cowboys, and some old bits of tentacle from the Pirates' Adventure with Squid, as well as several Post-it Notes reminding the Pirate Captain to say things like 'Splice the mainsail!' or 'Hard about, lads!' On the walls there hung several fantastic paintings of the Pirate Captain himself—one of them showed him looking anguished and cradling a dead swan: this painting was titled *WHY?* Another was of the Pirate Captain reclining naked except for a small piece of gauze. And a third pictured the Pirate Captain sharing a strange futuristic-looking drink with a lady who seemed to be made from metal. There were also

---

*'Shanty' probably derives from the French word *chanter*, meaning 'to sing'. Most shanties tended to be about frisky mermaids who loved putting out for sailors more than anyone.

quite a lot of nautical maps and charts about the place, and even an astrolabe. The Pirate Captain wasn't 100 per cent sure what the astrolabe did, or whether it was actually an astrolabe rather than a sextant, but he enjoyed fiddling with it when he got bored, nonetheless. Right at the moment boredom was an issue that weighed heavily on the Pirate Captain's mind.

'Care for some grog?' he asked politely. The scarf-wearing pirate wasn't very thirsty, but he said yes anyway, because if you start turning down grog when you're a pirate it doesn't help your reputation much.

'Ship's biscuits? I've got ship's custard creams, and ship's bourbons,' said the Pirate Captain. He held out a tin that had a boat painted on it and the pirate with a scarf took a bourbon, because he knew custard creams were the Pirate Captain's favourites.

'What do you think all that brawling was about, number two?' asked the Pirate Captain, absentmindedly seeing how fast he could spin the astrolabe using just one finger.

'Like the men said . . . it was just a friendly discussion that got a bit out of hand,' replied the scarf-wearing pirate, not entirely sure where the Pirate Captain was going with this, but amazed as always that he could carry on a conversation whilst doing complex calculations with an astrolabe. That sort of thing was why the Pirate Captain was the Pirate Captain, the pirate with a scarf reflected.

'I'll tell you what it was about,' said the Pirate Captain. 'It was about bored pirates! I've made a mistake. We've been moored here in . . . in the . . .' The Pirate Captain rubbed his nose, which he liked to think of as a stentorian nose, even though stentorian is actually a tone of voice, and squinted at one of the charts.

'The West Indies, sir,' said the scarf-wearing pirate, helpfully.

'Mmmm. Well, we've been here too long. I thought that after our exciting adventure with those cowboys, we could all do with a break, but I guess us pirates are only really happy when we're pirating.'

'I think you're right, sir,' the scarf-wearing pirate said. 'It's nice enough here, but I keep on finding sand in my grog, from all that lying about on the beach. And those native women, wandering about with no tops on . . . it's a bit much.'

'Exactly. It's time we had another pirate adventure!'

'I'll let the other pirates know. Where will we be heading for? Skull Island? The Spanish Main?'

'Oh, Lord, no! If we plunder the Spanish Main* one more time, I think I'll tear out my own beard,' said the Pirate Captain, trying on the ten-gallon hat and narrowing his eyes like a cowboy as he studied his reflection in the mirror.

---

*It was Francis Drake who had first made the Spanish Main a popular target, back in 1571. A replica of his boat, the *Golden Hind*, can be found today next to London Bridge.

'So what were you thinking?'

'Something will come up. It usually does. Just make sure we've got plenty of hams on board. I didn't really enjoy our last adventure much, because we ran out of hams about halfway through. And what's my motto? "I like ham!" '

'It's a good motto, sir.'

Back on deck, the other pirates had finished their shanty—which had been about how a beautiful sea-nymph had left her rich but stupid Royal Navy boyfriend for a pirate boyfriend because he was much more interesting to talk to and could make her laugh—and now they were roaring. This was another common pastime amongst the pirates.

'Rah!'

'Oooh-arg!'

'Aaaarrrr, me hearties!'

It didn't mean much, but it filled a few hours. They all stopped when they saw the pirate with a scarf had come back from his meeting with the Pirate Captain. He almost slipped in a pool of the cabin boy's blood that was left over from the fight.

'Can somebody swab these decks?' he said, a little tetchily. Left to their own devices, the pirates tended towards the bone idle.

'It's Tuesday! Sunday is boat cleaning day!'

'I know, but somebody could get hurt.'

The diffident pirate gave a shrug and went off to find a swabbing cloth, whilst the remaining crew looked up expectantly from where they were sprawled. The scarf-wearing pirate gazed out across the sparkling water, and at the tropical beach with its alabaster sands, and the forest of coconut palms behind that, and then he noticed one of the pretty native ladies and so he quickly looked back down at his pirate shoes.

'Listen up, pirates,' he said. 'I know all this endless wandering up and down the beach . . . and our inter-minable attempts at trying to choose which sort of mouth-watering exotic fruit to eat . . . and all these wanton tropical girls knocking around . . . I know it's been getting you down.'

A couple of the pirates muttered something to each other, but the scarf-wearing pirate didn't quite catch what they said.

'So you'll be happy to know,' he went on, 'that the Pirate Captain has ordered us to put to sea, just as soon as we've collected some hams for the journey.'

A buzz of excitement ran around the deck.

'Perhaps we should cook the hams first, before setting off?' asked the pirate dressed in green.

'That sounds like a good idea,' said the albino pirate.

'Do you think roasting is best?' asked the pirate with a nut allergy.

The scarf-wearing pirate sighed, because he knew how seriously the pirates took their ham, and he could predict how this was going to end up. He tried to look hard-nosed, which involved tensing all the muscles in his nostrils, and with as much authority as he could manage he said, 'Yes, roasting is good. It allows the free escape of watery particles that's necessary for a full flavour. But we've got to make sure it's regulated by frequent basting with the fat that has exuded from the meat, combined with a little salt and water—otherwise the hams will burn, and become hard and tasteless.'

'Roasting?* Are you sure?' asked the surly pirate who was dressed in red, barely concealing his contempt. 'What about boiling? I always find a boiled ham becomes more savoury in taste and smell, and more firm and digestible.'

'Ah, but if you continue the process too long, you risk the hams becoming tough and less succulent,' said the pirate in green.

'But the loss from roasting is upwards of twenty-two per cent of the ham! The loss from boiling is only about sixteen per cent. More ham for us! That can only be a good thing.'

'We need to dust the hams with bread raspings if we're going to boil them. And we should dress the knuckle bone with a frill of white paper.'

---

*In those days, roasting would have meant spit-roasting. A popular craze in the early part of the nineteenth century was to use a small dog fastened to a treadmill to turn the spit, freeing up the cook to prepare other dishes.

'A frill of white paper? What kind of a pirate are you? Rah!'

The pirates started to fight again, and it wasn't until one of them noticed that the Pirate Captain had come back from his cabin and was now leaning against the mast, drumming his fingers on a barrel, that they shuffled to attention.

'That's enough of that, my beauties!' he roared. 'Let's set a course'—at this point the Pirate Captain paused in what he hoped would be a dramatic and exciting fashion—'for adventure!'

The crew just gave him a bit of a collective blank look. The Pirate Captain sighed.

'All right,' he said with a pout, 'south.'

Two

RETURN TO
SKULL ISLAND!

'That was some hurricane!' said the pirate who was prone to exaggeration, emptying the seawater that had collected in his pirate boots over the side of the boat. 'I don't think I've ever seen one like it! I thought the mast was going to crack for sure! And we must have lost half a dozen men, just washed away into the deep.'*

'That wasn't a hurricane. It wasn't even a storm,' said the pirate in red.

'Well, gale then. That was some gale.'

'Pfft!' said the pirate in red. He was fed up, because a

---

*The Caribbean and the Gulf of Mexico were, and are, subject to devastating hurricanes. In 1712 Governor Hamilton reported that a storm had destroyed thirty-eight ships in the harbour at Port Royal and nine ships at Kingston.

whole day had gone by and they didn't seem to be any closer to actually starting an adventure.

'According to my Beaufort Scale,' said the albino pirate, waving a nautical pamphlet at the rest of the crew, 'a hurricane is number twelve, or "that which no canvas could withstand". As you can see, our canvases are fine, so it obviously wasn't a hurricane. I should say it was somewhere between number six, a Strong Breeze—or "that which will send a pirate's hat flying and muss up his luxuriant beard"—and number eight, a Fresh Gale—or "that which will make a pirate's trousers billow about so that it looks like he has fat legs".'

'Are you sure that's an actual Beaufort Scale you've got there?' asked the scarf-wearing pirate.

'Of course I'm sure,' snapped the albino pirate. 'The Pirate Captain wrote it out for me himself.'

All the pirates were too tired even to roar at each other, let alone sing a shanty, after their strenuous efforts in bringing the boat through the previous night's fantastic storm or fresh gale or strong breeze or whatever it happened to be. So they just sprawled on the deck, looking up at the last few seagulls to have made it this far out from land, circling above in what was now a clear blue sky. It wasn't until the smell of fresh ham wafted from the boat's kitchen that the pirates stirred and went below to the pirate dining room.

The Pirate Captain was already sitting at the table,

tapping his knife and fork expectantly. Of all the pirates, it was true that nobody loved his ham more than the Pirate Captain. The hams were brought to the table, and they had been roasted, which annoyed the pirate who had argued they should have been boiled, but he was so hungry he didn't bother to complain, and he had to admit that they tasted delicious. The pirates tore into their food and grog with the relish that comes from a hard night's pirating.

'Honestly, pirates! Have you forgotten that you are provided with teeth? Small wonder you complain about indigestion when you forget to chew!' admonished the Pirate Captain.

'I thought it was cold feet that gave you indigestion,' said the pirate with a hook where his hand should have been. 'And that wrapping your feet in a hot towel would prevent such belly pains.'

'That's headaches, idiot!' said the pirate in green.

'No. Headaches are most commonly caused from reading by candlelight, when the candle is positioned incorrectly. It should be placed behind you, so the rays can pass directly over your shoulder to the book.'

The pirates almost started fighting again over this, but the Pirate Captain held up an imperious hand and started to speak.

'I got a letter this morning,' he said, 'from our old enemy Black Bellamy.'

The pirates muttered a few oaths. Black Bellamy was

the roguish rival pirate whom the pirates had encoun-tered during the Pirates' Adventure with Buried Treasure and the Pirates' Adventure with the Princess of Cadiz. Somehow they weren't surprised that they had not heard the last of him.

'Black Bellamy has invited us to a feast on board his schooner, the *Barbary Hen,* which is sailing just a few leagues from here.'

'It's Black Bellamy, Captain! You can't mean to trust him!' said the albino pirate. The other pirates nodded.

'Perhaps he's changed,' said the Pirate Captain. 'He says in his letter that he's changed, and that he wants to hold this feast to make up for all the trouble he and his villainous crew have caused us in the past.'

'Oh, well. You can't really argue with that sort of sen-timent,' agreed the pirate in green.

'Yes, that seems really nice of him,' said the albino pirate, feeling a bit guilty for being so harsh on Black Bellamy just a few seconds ago.

'And it would be good to see how they prepare their hams on board the *Barbary Hen,*' added the pirate in red.

'So it's settled. We'll accept the invitation and set sail for Black Bellamy's feast at once!' said the Pirate Captain, picking a piece of ham from his immaculate beard.

The moonlit waters were clear and calm as the pirate boat moored up alongside the *Barbary Hen*. The pirate crew piled into a launch—'Shotgun!' shouted the sassy pirate who liked to sit up front with the Captain—and paddled across to where a rope-ladder had been hung over the other ship's side. There were around forty head of hog wandering about the darkened decks, which was clearly Black Bellamy's way of impressing his guests. Black Bellamy politely took the pirates' coats and cutlasses. This showed he really *had* changed, because the Black Bellamy of old was famous for his lack of manners. But he was still a fearsome sight, with a beard that came up to his eyes, two pairs of pistols hanging at the end of a silk sling, and a big knife held between his teeth.

'Herro. Relcon ahord ha *Harrarry Hen*,' said Black Bellamy.

'What did he say?' whispered the pirate in green.

'I think he said, "Welcome aboard the *Barbary Hen*." It's a bit hard to tell, because of that knife clenched between his teeth,' said the scarf-wearing pirate.

Black Bellamy made a few incomprehensible introductions, and then led the pirates into his feasting hall. Their old rival had certainly pulled out all the stops—there was roast veal, which had half a pint of melted butter poured over it, fillets of beef garnished with slices of lemon, a sumptuous pork broth, potato scones, stewed mushrooms . . . several of the pirates had to use their pirate neckerchiefs to wipe saliva from their mouths. It didn't matter that they had already eaten a sumptuous feast earlier that day, because they often had adventures comprised of nothing but sumptuous feasts. Initially, because there was so much history between them, the two sets of pirates were a bit hostile, and conversation was understandably awkward, but after some pirate grog they were soon carousing with each other. Piratical conversation buzzed about the boat.

'Diving. Have you ever tried it? It's fantastic! We went and dived at the wreck of an actual pirate ship!'

'My friend here thinks you should boil hams, but he's an idiot.'

'. . . 'twas the unmistakable tang of human flesh . . .'

'. . . and I'm not making this up—he had a wooden leg!'

Both Black Bellamy and the Pirate Captain were pleased it was going so well.

'Why don't we adjourn to my drawing room, for a spot of cards?* Hmmm?' said Black Bellamy to the Pirate Captain. The Pirate Captain could have gone on eating mutton necks all night, but his host had been so gracious he thought it rude to refuse.

---

*Captain Johnson's *General History of the Pyrates* tells us that most pirate ships had a set of Articles, by which the crew had to adhere. Article 3 states, 'No person to game at cards or dice for money', so Black Bellamy is showing his maverick colours here.

The pirates were a bit annoyed by how nice the drawing room was, especially when Black Bellamy flipped open the top of a huge mahogany globe to reveal a little drinks cabinet. The Pirate Captain's globe back on board the pirate boat was made out of tin and about the size of a football, and he wasn't even sure it had Africa on it, so it was difficult not to feel a pang of jealousy. Black Bellamy poured out some rum from a crystal decanter and suggested a game of Cincinnati High Low.

'Oh, that's a lucky man's game,' said the Pirate Captain, because he had heard someone say this before.

'Well, what would you suggest?' asked Black Bellamy amiably. 'Crossfire? Seven Card Flip? Mexican Seven Card Stud?'

He was just showing off, thought the Pirate Captain, but he was no slouch at cards himself.

'How about,' said the Pirate Captain, 'Cat's Cradle? Or Round the World? Or Walking the Dog?'

'Those are yo-yo tricks.'

'Ha! Of course they are. Well then, that one with the Mexicans.'

They settled down to the card game. Pretty soon the Pirate Captain was down several doubloons, and pretty soon after that he had lost all the boat's precious supply of hams. The trouble was that Black Bellamy's beard, coming up all the way to his eyes as it did, gave him a perfect poker face. The Pirate Captain's crew was starting to get worried, but then the Pirate Captain had a fantastic idea. He found himself with another useless hand but this time, instead of thumping the table and looking miserable, he gave a big grin, and whispered loudly to the pirate who wore a scarf, 'We'll be feasting on that forty head of hog, with this brilliant hand!'

Black Bellamy heard this, and decided to fold. The Pirate Captain shuffled the pile of doubloons into his pockets. Black Bellamy saw his cards and gasped.

'But . . . you had a terrible hand! Garbage!'

'Yes. But I knew that if I looked pleased with it, you would think it was a flush or something like that!'

'You're confounded clever!' roared Black Bellamy. 'But listen. Give me back all those doubloons I've just lost, and in return I'll tell you where you can find ten times that sort of loot.'

The Pirate Captain thought about Black Bellamy's offer for a second or two. Mathematics wasn't his strong point—obviously pirating was his strong point—but you didn't need to be Archimedes to realise that ten times the amount of doubloons he had just won was a good deal of cash.

'Very well, Black Bellamy,' said the Pirate Captain, taking the coins back out of his pockets. 'Where can we find this treasure?'

'I'll need to show you on the nautical charts,' sighed Black Bellamy, doing a sad face. 'Me and my men had been planning to sail to the South Seas, near the Galápagos Islands, where a ship belonging to the—uh—Bank of England is right this moment transporting . . . ooh, at least a hundred weight in gold bullion, back from the colonies. I'd been really looking forward to a spot of plundering, but I guess I'll just have to let you set about the raid yourself!'

'You're sure about this?' said the Pirate Captain, his eyes narrowing. 'That's eight hundred leagues from here. It's a little out of our way.'

'I swear by the Pirate Code.'

'Do you know the name of this ship?'

'It's called the *Beagle*. And it's chock full of gold, mark my words. Can I have those doubloons back now?'

As the pirates crossed back to their boat they could hear laughter coming from the *Barbary Hen*—it was good, thought the Pirate Captain, that they had left their hosts in such high spirits, even though he had got the better of Black Bellamy. And now he was pretty confident that they really *were* setting course . . . for adventure!

Though he didn't bother saying it out loud this time.

Three

PIRATE ISLANDS AND
BLACK-HEARTED MEN!

'So, there's two pirate boats sailing towards each other,' said the short pirate with thick black spectacles, 'and one of the boats is carrying all this blue paint. And the other pirate boat is carrying all this red paint. They crash, and you know what happened?'

'What happened?'

'They were marooned! Ha-ha! You see?'

The pirates had started telling each other jokes in an attempt to ward off the inevitable boredom between feasts, because there wasn't much else to do on board a pirate boat. They had been at sea for a couple of days now, searching high and low for the *Beagle*. When the boat had first reached the tropical waters surrounding the Galápagos Islands the pirates kept themselves amused by capturing a couple of the giant turtles that frequented this part of the world, and then racing them about the deck.* You could fit two whole pirates on each shell. They constructed an obstacle course from bits of old rope and rigging, but the turtles proved a lot less resilient than they had hoped. A few of the pirates then had the bright idea that if they caught enough of the huge diaphanous jellyfish that circled about the boat, they could construct a kind of bouncy castle. This kept them occupied for a few more hours, but it didn't really work, and eventually they got tired of it, and found that they had jellyfish guts stuck all over their pirate boots.

The pirate dressed in green went downstairs to get a glass of water because he was nervous and his throat was dry. There was a note stuck next to the ship's sink, written in the Pirate Captain's familiar bubble writing. It read:

Will whoever keeps taking my mug STOP IT. *It is very annoying. Have a little respect for other people's property.*

The Pirate Captain

Life at sea was tough and unforgiving, and tensions could run quite high on board a pirate boat, especially when crockery was limited and people didn't always do

---

*Nowadays Galápagos Giant Turtles often accidentally eat plastic bags left as litter by unthinking tourists, mistaking them for tasty jellyfish.

their washing-up, but generally the pirates all got along fine. The pirate dressed in green gulped down the tap water—it was much nicer than seawater—and tried to pluck up courage for the task ahead. He'd been putting it off for ages, but now seemed as good a time as any.

There was a knock at the Pirate Captain's door, and then the pirate in green came in.

'Sorry to be bothering you, Captain,' he said. The Pirate Captain looked up. He had a lot to sort out in preparation for their imminent and audacious attack, but he made a point of always having time for the men.

'What can I do for you . . . uh . . . my fellow?' said the Pirate Captain, who often found it difficult to tell his crew apart from one another. 'Grog? Ham?'

'No thanks, sir. I was wondering if I could ask you something?'

'It's what I'm here for. You don't mind if I help myself?' said the Pirate Captain, indicating the slices of ham. 'Now, what is it?'

'Well, I was thinking of getting a tattoo.'

'They're quite popular.'

'Yes, Captain.'

'But they don't come off, you know.'

'Yes, Captain. I've thought about that.'

'Well then.'

'I thought it might be good to get a Skull and Crossbones, like we have on our flag, but it turns out a couple of the men have already got that. So . . . I was wondering . . . that's to say . . . would you have any objections . . .'

'Spit it out, man!'

'. . . if I got your face done instead? I was thinking of adding a little speech bubble, with—ha—you saying "Scurvy knaves!" like you always do. It would be on my arm, if that's all right.' He indicated the patch on his upper arm where he was going to have the tattoo.

For a moment, the Pirate Captain was speechless. The ham on his fork just hung in mid air.

'Of course . . . I . . . ah . . . I don't know what to say,' he said.

'Are you okay, Captain?'

'Yes . . . it's just this, um, ham. It's very spicy, and it's making my eyes water.'

In all their many adventures, even the one where they had battled zombie pirates, the Pirate Captain had never been so touched by a gesture from any of his loyal pirate crew. His lip began to tremble, and the pirate in green was mightily relieved when at that point the pirate with an accordion, breathless with excitement, hurried into the Captain's office.

'Sorry to interrupt, Captain, but we've caught sight of a ship, and we think it's the *Beagle,* because it has a funny-looking dog painted on the side. Should I get the men ready for boarding?'

The Pirate Captain swiftly regained his composure, and started to bark out orders. 'Get the cannons ready first, and remind the pirates not to stand right behind them this time,' he bellowed. The Pirate Captain had explained basic Newtonian physics and the principles of recoil to his men more times than he could remember, but it just didn't seem to go in.

'And I want to hear plenty of roaring until we've secured the enemy vessel,' he said, picking up a telescope and marching onto the deck, where several of the pirates were already gathered.

'It's just a ten-gun brig,' said the scarf-wearing pirate, scratching thoughtfully at a livid scar that ran the length of his cheek. On most people a scar can be quite disfiguring, but several of the pirates thought that in the pirate with a scarf's case it actually added to his rather rugged appeal.

'A ten-gun brig? Really?' said the Pirate Captain, frowning at the news.

'I was expecting something bigger, seeing as it's carrying all this gold for the Bank of England,' said his number two.

'Perhaps they're trying to keep a low profile,' said the Pirate Captain, with some misgivings. 'Are those cannons ready?'

'This sort of makes us bank robbers, doesn't it?'

'Aaarrr. But you knew you'd be bending a few laws when you became a pirate. I'm not sure the ivory smuggling we were doing the other week was entirely respectable. Or all that trawling for cod, come to think about it.'

'Cannons ready, Captain.'

An eerie silence suddenly becalmed the pirate chatter, as the crew waited for the Pirate Captain to give his order to make good the attack.

'Fire a cannonball at that boat!' said the Pirate Captain.

Four

WHAT EVIL
LURKS IN THE
UNFORGIVING DEEP?

'Confound it, man!' said Robert FitzRoy, captain of the boat about to be attacked by the pirates. 'I told you women and the sea were a mighty bad combination.'

FitzRoy was young for a ship's captain, just twenty-seven, but the man he stood back to back with was younger still, a full five years his junior. Yet neither bore the frisky demeanour that you would expect to find in people under thirty.

'I can't help myself, Robert,' said his companion, Charles Darwin, cradling his big round head in his hands. 'I love her, and I mean to marry her!'

'But I love her too!' said FitzRoy. 'She drives me to distraction! You already knew that.'

'Damn women, with . . . with their hair . . . and their faces . . . ,' muttered Darwin.

'I must demand satisfaction,' said Captain FitzRoy. 'You don't leave me any choice.'

The cabin was a little small for a duel, neither man quite being able to stand up properly without grazing his head, but needs must at sea.

'Three years' voyage . . . and it should come to this,' said Darwin, shakily pouring powder into his pistol. 'May the best man win.'

'You're a botanist.* I'm a trained naval officer. I don't fancy your chances much,' said FitzRoy.

The door was flung open with a crash that made Darwin wince, and in ran the breathless cause of the two men's argument, the lovely Lady Mara. 'Please stop!' she said with her lovely mouth. 'There's—'

But before Lady Mara could say any more, a cannonball splintered through the cabin wall at tremendous speed, and buried itself in the side of her pretty head, knocking her off her feet, and leaving her quite dead on the floor. Darwin and FitzRoy stood, dumbfounded.

---

*Darwin was serving as an unpaid naturalist on board the HMS *Beagle*. The *Beagle* was unimpressive for its day—just ninety feet long and of a notoriously unseaworthy design. In his notes Darwin described the voyage as 'one continual puke'.

'Well. I . . .'

'Should we . . . ?' Darwin gestured at his gun.

'Hardly seems much point.'

'What a damned fool I've been!' laughed Darwin.

'Oh, I'm just as much to blame,' said FitzRoy with a grin, pocketing his pistol, and slapping his friend on the back. They would have hugged right there and then, but were interrupted by a further crash as first another cannonball and then a pirate screamed in through the window. The two men stood stock-still.

'Don't make any sudden movements,' whispered Fitz-Roy to his companion. 'Remember—he's more scared of us than we are of him.'

'That's bears, you idiot,' hissed Darwin out of the side of his mouth. 'I don't think it applies to pirates.'

At the doorway, a second pirate appeared, with a luxuriant beard and a pleasant, open face, all teeth and curls.

'I'm the Pirate Captain. And I'm here for the gold!' he said.

Everybody froze. For a moment the only sound was the gentle roar of the ocean, and some wheezing from the pirate with asthma.

'Well, uh, help yourself,' said FitzRoy eventually, slightly perplexed. Darwin was too terrified to speak.

'Not that there's a great deal,' continued the young

captain. 'I think some of the portholes might be made of gold, but then again they could be made of brass. Same sort of colour, so it's difficult to tell.'

'Rah!' said the Pirate Captain, with a frightful bellow. 'I know you're carrying a hundred weight in gold bullion!'

'Really?' said FitzRoy, genuinely surprised. 'I haven't seen anything of the sort.'

'Perhaps the bit of boat that's under the water is made of gold,' ventured Darwin, finding his voice at last. 'I mean, it could be made of anything for all we know. You never get to see it.'

The Pirate Captain's icy blade against his throat struck him silent.

'Search the hold, men, and bring me back some gold,' said the Pirate Captain, with a sneer reminiscent of Elvis.

The pirates were pretty slick by this stage of their piratical careers, and they had managed to overrun the entire ship in a matter of minutes. The only casualty on the pirate side had been the pirate dressed in red, who had twisted his ankle trying to do that trick where you slide down the face of the mainsail, cutting it as you go with your cutlass—which worked fine up to a point but still left a twenty-foot drop once he reached the bottom of the canvas.

'Ouch! My ankle!' he cried, but none of the other pirates had much sympathy for his reckless showboating. A group of them headed into the hold—but instead of the clinking you would associate with gold, all they could hear was the chatter of creatures. One of the pirates tore at a tarpaulin, only to discover row upon row of cages, each containing some sort of monkey.

'The gold must be hidden inside these monkeys!' shouted a pirate. Several of the pirates put down their flickering lamps, picked up monkeys of various different types, and slit them end to end, but all that spilt out was monkey guts.

'Gold!' said the pirate with an accordion, holding something yellowish up hopefully.

'That's not gold. It's a gall bladder,' said the pirate with a hook for his hand.

Covered in bits of creature, and thoroughly dejected, the pirate crew tramped back to FitzRoy's cabin.

'Pieces of ape! Pieces of ape!' squawked Gary, the ship's parrot.

'Will somebody shut him up?' scowled the pirate in green.

'There's no treasure here, Captain. Just a lot of stupid creatures,' said the pirate with a scarf.

'Just like I told you,' said FitzRoy.

The Pirate Captain sat down and rubbed his eyes with a weary hand. It suddenly felt like it had been a very long day.

'But Black Bellamy . . . he said you were carrying gold for the Bank of England.'

'The Bank of England?' said FitzRoy, grabbing at a table as the *Beagle* started to list alarmingly. 'I believe I've heard there is such a boat. But it's sailing in the vicinity of the West Indies, from what I remember.'

'The West Indies? But that's where we've just come from!'

'That Black Bellamy!' said the pirate with a hook instead of a hand. 'He was just trying to get us out of the way, so that he could plunder it for himself! Why, he hasn't changed at all! We've been bamboozled!'

The pirates were all very disappointed with the way Black Bellamy had behaved.

'So, then. Um. What are you doing in these parts?' said the Pirate Captain to Darwin, trying to make a bit of lighthearted conversation, and feeling more than a little awkward now.

'We're on a scientific expedition.'

'Searching for creatures?'

'I have a theory,' said Darwin, looking serious. 'I'm afraid it's proved to be rather controversial. We came here looking for proof.'

'What is this theory? In terms a pirate might understand.'

'It is not something to be taken lightly. It will make you look at the world with fresh eyes. Things may never seem the same again,' said Darwin, in a spooky voice.

'Go on,' said the Pirate Captain, his curiosity bitten.

Darwin gave a dramatic pause.

'In short, I believe that a monkey, properly trained, given the correct dietary regime, and dressed in fancy clothes, can be made indistinguishable from a human gentleman. I believe he would cease to be a monkey, and become more a . . . a Man-panzee, if you will.'

A silence held the room. One of the pirates whistled.

'I . . . see. A Man-panzee?' said the Pirate Captain.

'But because of my outlandish theories I have made some powerful enemies—primarily, the Bishop of Oxford,' said Darwin, unable to keep the bitterness out of his voice.

'He finds it offensive?'

'He most certainly does!'

'Because it contravenes his religious beliefs?'

'Oh no! Nothing to do with that, my dear Pirate Captain. The Bishop of Oxford recently became the largest shareholder in P. T. Barnum's world-famous Circus of Freaks.' Darwin leant forward with a conspiratorial air. 'The circus has been making a killing of late, because all of London Town is entranced by its latest exhibit . . . the fantastical Elephant Man. Have you heard of him?'

'Aarrr. He was on show last time we were in England,' said the Pirate Captain. 'A real disappointment as I remember. Doesn't even have a trunk. The trick is not to treat him like a gentleman, because he always starts crying if you do that.'

'Anyhow, the Bishop of Oxford is clearly alarmed that my Man-panzee might steal his Elephant Man's thunder. So he denounced my ideas as blasphemous—he even said there was a bit in the Bible about how it was a sin to dress a monkey up in a waistcoat, but when asked for the page reference, he claimed to have forgotten.'

Darwin was clearly on the verge of an angry rage.

'So I joined this expedition in an attempt to find a suitable specimen. Only now I have received word from England that my brother Erasmus has gone missing! I believe he has been kidnapped by the Bishop of Oxford as a means of safeguarding against my successful return. I fear the Bishop intends to do him some great harm unless I abandon my research.'

'Does that mean you've had some success?' asked one of the pirates.

'Come, let me show you.'

Darwin and FitzRoy led the pirates to an adjoining cabin. The pirates gasped, for though the room was dark and cramped, they could still make out its sole occupant. Sitting in a leather-backed armchair was a monkey with the best posture any of the pirates had ever seen. Dressed in an expensive-looking silk suit, with a pipe in his mouth, the creature peered at the pirates through a gold-rimmed monocle. He appeared to be sipping on some sort of cocktail—the Pirate Captain thought he could smell gin. The monkey looked as if he had been freshly shaved, but he was still recognisably a monkey, though if you squinted he might have passed for a wizened old man, or a gigantic walnut.

'Obviously he cannot talk,' said Darwin, turning on a few gaslights. 'But he is able to carry on a conversation by use of flash cards. Though I expect that sometime in the future, technology will move on, so that rather than having to rely on the cards he'll be able to use . . . oh, I don't know, refrigerator magnets, something like that.'

The monkey straightened his cravat, and held up a series of cards in quick succession.

| HELLO | THERE | PIRATES | PLEASED | TO | MEET |

| YOU | he spelt out. | MY | NAME | IS | MISTER | BOBO |

'Erm, pleased to meet you too,' said the Pirate Captain, who, truth be told, felt like an idiot talking to a monkey, even one as finely dressed as this.* He turned to Darwin, 'It's a fantastic achievement.'

'Yes, Mister Bobo is by far my most promising specimen. I'm glad you didn't hit him with a cannonball. Please, let me give you a demonstration.' Darwin turned to the dapper little creature. 'Mister Bobo, would you tell us how one goes about being a proper gentleman?'

---

*You share about 98.6 per cent of your DNA with a common chimpanzee. And upwards of 99 per cent of your DNA with a pirate!

The monkey appeared deep in thought, and then shuffled through his pack of flash cards.

MODERATION DECORUM AND NEATNESS

DISTINGUISH THE GENTLEMAN. HE IS AT

ALL TIMES AFFABLE DIFFIDENT AND STUDIOUS

TO PLEASE. INTELLIGENT AND POLITE, HIS

BEHAVIOUR IS PLEASANT AND GRACEFUL.

WHEN HE ENTERS THE DWELLING OF AN

INFERIOR, HE ENDEAVOURS TO HIDE IF

POSSIBLE THE DIFFERENCE BETWEEN THEIR

RANKS OF LIFE. EVER WILLING TO ASSIST

THOSE AROUND HIM, HE IS NEITHER

UNKIND HAUGHTY NOR OVERBEARING. IN THE

MANSIONS OF THE RICH THE CORRECTNESS

OF HIS MIND INDUCES HIM TO BEND TO

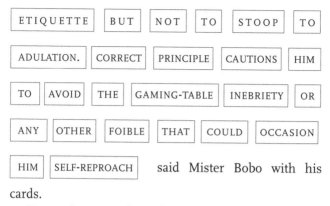

ETIQUETTE BUT NOT TO STOOP TO ADULATION. CORRECT PRINCIPLE CAUTIONS HIM TO AVOID THE GAMING-TABLE INEBRIETY OR ANY OTHER FOIBLE THAT COULD OCCASION HIM SELF-REPROACH said Mister Bobo with his cards.

'You see? Not exactly perfect, but he makes a good stab at it. For a monkey,' said Darwin.

Flash cards were hardly the fastest way of communicating, and by now the pirates' bellies were rumbling. Also their pirate boots were getting wet as the *Beagle* started to sink, so they'd been hoping that the young scientist might have finished his speech, but Darwin, obviously proud of his discovery, went on.

'Naturally, I intended to find a better class of tailor back in England, one who might be able to do something to conceal his huge unsightly ass.'

'It *is* a big ass,' agreed a pirate.

'How have you been able to train him so well?' asked the Pirate Captain.

'Mostly fire.' Darwin nodded at some hot tongs hanging on the wall, and Mister Bobo looked a bit frightened. 'But it's all been a waste. I'll never be able to show him off to high society, for fear of some terrible retribution suffered by Erasmus. And even if I did intend to confront the black-hearted Bishop of Oxford, now I don't even have a means of returning home to England. I am lost.'

And with that Darwin started to bawl like a baby. The pirates stared at the floor, and shifted from foot to foot. They couldn't help but feel a little responsible for the scientist's predicament, on account of their scuppering his boat with all those cannonballs. The pirates had a bit of a discussion amongst themselves. Then the Pirate Captain turned to Darwin.

'I don't much care to be hung in irons.* And that's what we've been promised if we ever set foot in England again. But we don't want to see you and your Manpanzee bested by this scoundrel Bishop you've told us about. So just as soon as we've eaten, us pirates will help you rescue your brother, and get Mister Bobo accepted by Victorian high society and everything.'

Darwin went to plant a big kiss on the Pirate Captain's salty face, but then thought better of it and shook him by the hand. Everybody cheered, even Mister Bobo.

---

*As a warning to seafarers it was common practice in Britain and her overseas colonies to put the bodies of notorious pirates on display near the entrance to a port. Several pirates were hanged at Execution Dock on the banks of the Thames in London.

Five

TRAPPED IN QUICKSAND!

The pirates helped Darwin, FitzRoy, and the crew of the *Beagle* shift their luggage from the slowly sinking boat.

'You'll have to sleep in a hammock, I'm afraid,' said the Pirate Captain. 'They're quite comfortable, but they can leave a criss-cross pattern on your buttocks.'

'Are you sure there's room?' asked Darwin, anxious not to be too much trouble.

'Don't worry about that. We'll make room,' said the Pirate Captain, adding with a merry wink, 'Truth is I've been meaning to have some of my pirates walk the plank for ages, I just haven't got round to it.'*

---

*Plank-walking as a punishment was nothing like as common as TV and films would suggest, but there is one report from *The Times* of 23 July 1829 of Dutch sailors being compelled to walk the plank by pirates from Buenos Aires.

'Walk the plank? That's barbaric!' blurted out Darwin, before remembering that pirate ways are not necessarily the ways of other men. 'I'm sorry, it's just . . . there's really no need to go to those lengths. We'll sleep standing up, like bats.'

The Pirate Captain swatted his objections away.

'Honestly, it's been far too long since we did this. Lately, if a pirate has been annoying us, we've just shaved off an eyebrow or drawn a little moustache on his face whilst he sleeps, but it's no real substitute.'

He rummaged about in a large pine box that one of the crew had fetched from the hold.

'Oh, I haven't seen those for a while!' said the Captain, pulling out a garish pair of old pirate trousers. 'What was I thinking?! Ah, here it is.'

He blew the dust off a big plank of wood. Seeing that Darwin and FitzRoy were still looking a bit concerned, the Pirate Captain shot them a reassuring grin.

'Listen,' he said. 'It's not like I make any old pirate take the terrible walk. Strictly fools and lubbers. It's for the good of the species.'

As soon as the pirate boat reached shark-infested waters, the Pirate Captain, with a steely glint in his eye, gave the order to drop anchor. There was a carnival atmosphere on board once the pirates realised that there was going to be some plank-walking. Darwin and FitzRoy looked on aghast as the Pirate Captain called out the first name.

The ratty-haired pirate called Marcus was the first to go. He begged and pleaded and cried like a little girl, but a few cutlass prods from some of the other pirates soon had him edging along the narrow piece of wood. He stopped at the end, and began to blubber again, so the pirate with a scarf crept up behind him, and quickly pushed him into the sea. The remaining pirates crowded round the edge of the deck, craning their necks to see ratty-haired Marcus desperately splashing about. For a bit, nothing much happened, but all of a sudden the water around him seemed to churn and crash in on itself, there was a scream, a cracking sound, and then a cloud of red spread out like a flower over the blue sea. The cloud of red wasn't a flower—it was blood coming out of Marcus. The pirates all gave a mighty cheer.*

The other pirates singled out by the harsh but undeniably fair Pirate Captain were dispatched in similar fashion. They included the balding archaeologist pirate called Stan; the rich pirate who tried to pass himself off as a hippy, whose name the Pirate Captain had forgotten; the pirate who had taught the Pirate Captain geography at Pirate Academy; a boring pirate from Oxford called Adam; and the stupid pirate who had got in the Pirate

---

*Despite the fearsome reputation of sharks, more people are actually killed each year by pigs. Also, sharks have no bones—their skeletons are made entirely from cartilage.

Captain's way when he was trying to eat pancakes. A late addition was a male model pirate whom the Pirate Captain hadn't even met.

As soon as the plank-walking was finished, the Pirate Captain pointed the boat towards England, and all the remaining pirates and their guests went belowdecks for a feast. For a change the pirates had lamb instead of ham, with the usual accompaniment of green mint sauce and a salad. As a nice added touch the roast lamb was sprinkled with a little minced parsley. A few of Darwin's monkeys had also been served up as an appetiser. There had been some debate as to the best way to cook a monkey, but eventually the pirates had decided to treat the monkeys as if they were turkeys, so after the sinews had been drawn from the legs and thighs, and the monkeys carefully trussed, they were stuffed with sausage meat and veal. It was all served with gravy and bread sauce. Too late the Pirate Captain realised that he had invited Mister Bobo to the feast, but if the creature was put out at being offered a slice of his chimpanzee brethren he was far too polite to say anything.

'So . . . have you been a pirate captain long?' asked Darwin, gulping down a mug of grog.

'Goodness me! Long as I can remember,' said the Pirate Captain.

'You've never considered as a career something a little more orthodox?'

'I dare say I've considered it, but the fact is I'm a slave to pirating! I love it! The salty sea air, the exotic locations, the shiny gold. Especially the shiny gold.'

'I can see you're pretty good at it,' said Darwin graciously. Pirates seemed a lot more civilised than he had expected. He was unaware of the tremendous effort most of the crew were making in an attempt to eat in a respectable manner because they didn't want to look sloppy in front of visitors. Several of them were wearing their most jaunty sashes, and they had spent all day cleaning the boat from top to bottom.

'I have to say,' said Darwin, looking misty-eyed, 'a part of me is quite jealous of your villainous lifestyle. Free from the tyranny of what society deems acceptable! Masters of your own fate! Living beyond the law! Us scientific types must seem rather dull to your piratical eyes.'

'Not at all,' said the Pirate Captain to his guest. 'I've always been interested in science. Perhaps, as a scientist, you'll be able to answer a question that has perplexed me for many years.'

'I'll certainly do my best.'

'Tell me—scientifically speaking—who do you think the tallest pirate in the world is?'

'Erm. It's a bit outside my field of expertise,' replied Darwin apologetically.

'Ah well. Perhaps I'm destined never to know!' said the Pirate Captain with a wistful air.

'Darwin's not the only one with a scientific theory,' said FitzRoy. 'I've been doing some fascinating work to do with weather prediction. I hope to found a meteorological office when I return to London.'

Nobody at the table was at all interested in what FitzRoy was talking about, so he trailed off and stared miserably at his soup.*

Darwin chewed on a monkey's paw. 'How long do you expect it will take us to reach England?'

'There's plenty of hams on board, if that's what you're worried about,' replied the Pirate Captain reassuringly. 'But let's see now . . .' The Captain gazed into the middle distance and furrowed his brow to make it look like he was doing some difficult calculations in his head. In fact he was wondering if anybody had noticed how shiny his boots were, because he'd had the pirate with a scarf spend the whole morning polishing them. 'I should say we'd reach England by Tuesday or thereabouts, with a decent wind behind us. It would be a lot quicker than that if we could just sail straight there, but I was looking at the nautical charts, and it's a good job I did, because it turns out there's a dirty great sea serpent right in the middle of the ocean! It has a horrible gaping maw and

---

*In 1865 FitzRoy committed suicide at his home in Upper Norwood. In 1862 he had published *The Weather Book*.

one of those scaly tails that looks like it could snap a boat clean in two. So I thought it best to sail around that.'

FitzRoy frowned. 'I think they just draw those on maps to add a bit of decoration. It doesn't actually mean there's a sea serpent there.'

The galley went rather quiet. A few of the pirate crew stared intently out of the portholes, embarrassed at their Captain's mistake. But to everyone's relief, instead of running somebody through, the Pirate Captain just narrowed his eyes thoughtfully.

'That explains a lot,' he said. 'I suppose it's also why we've never glimpsed that giant compass in the corner of the Atlantic. I have to say, I'm a little disappointed.'

Darwin thoughtfully picked a piece of macaque from between his teeth. 'You know, this reminds me of the time I was first searching for monkeys, on a nameless isle somewhere off the coast of South America,' he said, a far-off look in his eyes. 'It was close to Christmas, and the others in my expedition had been wanting to get home to their families and loved ones, but I was sure we were near to success, so I insisted that we stay. For several more days my search continued in vain, until I stumbled across a single severed monkey's claw in the heart of the steaming jungle. At last I had proof that there were monkeys to be found in the region, and I took the claw back to show the others. The rest of the expedition said it was disgusting and probably diseased, and they complained that I hadn't found a single complete monkey in six months. Once again they demanded that we should set sail, but I knew that in their heart of hearts they would be as disappointed as myself to return home empty-handed. So I ordered them to stay another month. But that very night strange and terrible things began to happen.'

'What sort of things?' asked the sassy pirate, wide-eyed.

'Strange messages appeared. The words "Darwin is an idiot" were written on my sleeping bag. My toothpaste went missing, and so did my shoes. Then, a few days later, I awoke to find all my fellow scientists gone, vanished as if into thin air, and the food and boat with them. If it hadn't been for a passing freighter, I might have perished on that godforsaken isle. I realised at once that the monkey's claw must carry a terrible curse, so I flung it back into the jungle from whence it came.'

'What had happened to the others in your expedition?'

'The strangest thing of all. When I returned to England I found the rest of the expedition sipping cocktails in our gentlemen's club. They seemed very surprised to see me. It turns out that they could have sworn they had told me they were setting sail, but when they realised I wasn't aboard it was too late, and for some strange reason they had all forgotten the way back to the island. I told them about the curse of the claw and they all agreed that must have been the cause of my misfortune.'

'What happened to the claw?' asked the Pirate Captain fearfully.

'We may never know...,' said Darwin, making a creepy face. The candles flickered eerily, and the shadows seemed to draw in around the room. His frightening story finished, the pirates looked at each other nervously. None of them was keen to get to bed.

'Well, good night.'

'Night.'

'What was that? Can you hear creaking?'

'We're on a boat, there's always creaking.'

'Ha! Yes. Of course. That must be it.'

'What a stupid story that man told.'

'It was stupid, wasn't it?'

Six

PIRATES AHOY!

After a brief encounter with some lovely but black-hearted lady pirates,* the pirate boat finally arrived in the sleepy seaside town of Littlehampton, on the south coast of England. Houses were still cheap there, compared to London prices, but of course there was always the risk of flooding. The beach was pretty good, and there was a lot of that seaweed that looks a bit like brains lying about. A couple of the pirates did impressions of the zombie pirates and said, 'Brains! Feed me brains!' and pretended to stuff the seaweed into their mouths.

'We must make haste to London,' said Darwin, fetching his suitcase up onto the beach, 'to meet my fellow scientists at the Royal Society.'

---

*Lady pirates were rare but not unheard of. A famous example was Anne Bonny, who became the lover of Calico Jack and was tried for piracy in Spanish Town, Jamaica.

'Yes, quite right. Not a moment to lose!' agreed the Pirate Captain. 'Except a few of the men noticed an amusement arcade just along from here, and I promised them they could go. It has a gigantic slide and everything.'

'But Erasmus! He could be in all sorts of danger!'

The Pirate Captain's eyes flashed red like hot cannonballs.

'I'm sure your brother wouldn't begrudge my crew a little entertainment after such a hard voyage,' he said, a hint of steel in his voice.

'Oh, very well,' replied Darwin, sulkily.

The pirate crew were excited to be visiting an arcade, but it proved to be a dilapidated affair. The only halfway decent machines consisted of an ingenious mechanical series of shelves, which all shunted backwards and forwards, each shelf laden with piles of silvery doubloons. By putting a doubloon into a little slot the hope was to knock several doubloons over the edge of a precipice, where they could be collected. The pirates spent ages on one of the machines, because there was an actual pocketwatch resting on the doubloons near the edge, but no matter how much of their treasure they fed into the gaspowered beast, the loot wouldn't fall down—it was almost as if the doubloons were stuck there with glue. A couple of the pirates got into trouble for trying to shake the machine, and they had to run outside and hide behind a man selling ice creams.

'This is rubbish,' said the pirate who was eating some candy floss, and the other pirates agreed, so they walked back down the beach to where Darwin and FitzRoy were waiting. Seeing them, Darwin leapt to his feet and gathered up his luggage once more.

'So, are we ready? There is a locomotive to London that leaves in half an hour,' said Darwin, eager to be off.

'Yes,' said the Pirate Captain. 'We must hurry! Oh look—a nautical-themed crazy golf! Let's have a go!'

'But the train . . . ,' said Darwin, with a touch of resignation.

'Nautical-themed! Do you think that's a genuine ship's anchor? It's very realistic. You and FitzRoy can play as a team if you want,' said the Pirate Captain, handing him a putter.

Darwin could see there was no point arguing with the Pirate Captain once he had made up his mind.

The Pirate Captain swung his golf club, and the ball pinged away, only to hit the side of a big metal anchor and roll back to where it had started.

'That's lucky, it's a free drop,' said the Pirate Captain, picking up his ball and placing it about a foot from the hole. 'Because I hit the anchor.'

'Eh? Are you sure about that?' asked Darwin, instantly wishing he had kept quiet.

'Yes. Because I hit the anchor,' repeated the Pirate Captain, this time in a menacing tone that spoke of rum and murder.

The pirate with a scarf hit his ball, which bounced off a barrel, hit the anchor, and rolled back again. He went to pick it up.

'What do you think you're doing?' roared the Pirate Captain incredulously.

'My free drop. Because I hit the anchor.'

'But you hit the barrel first!'

'Erm . . . yes.'

'So that invalidates any effect the anchor might have.'

'Oh.'

'And by hitting the barrel and then the anchor, you've put the anchor permanently out of play for everybody else. So no more free drops, I'm afraid.'

In all, they played three rounds of crazy golf and the Pirate Captain won all three, but everyone had a good time. As they ambled back along the sea front, the Pirate Captain told them all an exciting story about the time he lost a leg in a fight with a Great White Shark. FitzRoy remarked that the Pirate Captain seemed to have two perfectly good legs, at which point the Pirate Captain went a bit quiet and pretended to be very interested in a shell he had picked up.

'We'd better be off to rescue my brother,' said Darwin.

'Yes,' said the Pirate Captain. 'We shall. Just as soon as we've paid a visit to that sweet factory to find out how they get the words inside sticks of rock. Aargh! I'm just pulling your leg. Don't look so worried. I've sailed the seven seas, and I've never had an unsuccessful adventure yet!'

'Really? You've sailed all seven seas?' asked Darwin admiringly.

'Every last one!'

'What *are* the seven seas? I've always wondered.'

'Aaarrr. Well, let's see . . . ,' said the Pirate Captain, scratching his craggy forehead. 'There's the North Sea. And that other one, the one near Mozambique. And . . . what's that one in Hyde Park?'

'The Serpentine?'

'That's the one. How many's that, then? Three. Um. There's the sea with all the rocks in it . . . I think they call it Sea Number Four. Then that would leave . . . uh . . . Grumpy and Sneezy . . .'

Darwin was starting to look a little less impressed.

'Would you look at that big seagull!' said the Pirate Captain, quickly ducking into a beach hut.

Seven

TARGET: PIRATES!

A nd so the pirates and their companions arrived in Victorian London. It was not the London you would recognise from nowadays—there was no Millennium Wheel or Tate Modern or Eurostar or Starbucks or Millennium Dome or Jubilee Line Extension or any of the other things you probably assume have always existed. There was soot and orphans everywhere, and gaslit cobbled streets full of fog and sinister gentlemen out for a night of illicit murder. It was a strict and unforgiving society; looking at a piano, eating too much butter, dancing with elan—the sour-faced Queen Victoria forbade all these things. Also, it was always raining in the London of themadays—dirty grey slabs of rain that left everywhere shining and slippery.

To Darwin's continued dismay the Pirate Captain insisted they visit London Zoo before doing anything else. All the pirates agreed that it wasn't as good as Berlin Zoo, which they had visited on a previous adventure to Germany, and that it had far too large a hoofed-animals section. 'Who cares about hoofed animals? They never get up to anything!' said the pirate in green, wisely. The chimps were an especially sorry bunch—the chimps in Berlin Zoo had put on quite a display when the pirates had visited, shouting and weeing right in front of shocked tourists, but the London chimps just rocked back and forth, obviously suffering from zoo-psychosis. Mister Bobo stared sadly at them through the glass, a bit embarrassed on their behalf. The albino pirate noticed a sign which pointed to an exhibit of 'The Most Destructive Animal in the World!' Some of the pirates had bets on whether it would be a bear or a shark, but it turned out to be a big mirror. The most destructive animal in the world was mankind itself! Especially pirates! But to show they weren't all bad, two of the pirates decided to sponsor a polar bear.*

After that, even though Darwin kept on looking pointedly at his watch and rolling his eyes, the pirates went shopping in the West End. Several of them got themselves the latest pirate stylings from Carnaby Street. Apparently that year's fashion could be summed up as

---

*London Zoo is still going today, and this year's baby-bear-naming competition was won by Sandokan Soloman for his name, 'Ursula'.

'the more buckles the better!' and the pirates now made a loud clanking noise as they walked along. They also all bought a few postcards and Union Jacks. The pirate in green who wanted to have the Pirate Captain drawn on his arm had managed to find a tattoo parlour in the Soho district, and now carried a bundle of pamphlets with titles like 'Inky Skin', which he said he'd picked up because he was now very interested in tattoos, and not because of the pictures of ladies wearing next to nothing, but the other pirates weren't sure they believed him.

As they trailed down Charing Cross Road, finally exhausted from their exciting day out in the Big Smoke, the Pirate Captain noticed a poster stuck to a pillar box. It said in olden-days writing:

P.T. BARNUM
(in association with the Bishop of Oxford)
is proud to present his
W O R L D - F A M O U S
Circus of Freaks
featuring the Elephant Man! The Mermaid! A Beard of Bees!
Tuesday, Wednesday, Thursday, Friday and Saturday
are
'Ladies' Nights!' <u>Free entry all day to ladies.</u>

'That's a lot of ladies' nights,' said the Pirate Captain thoughtfully.

'Yes,' said Darwin. 'It's a peculiar thing. I heard from my cousin that ever since the Bishop of Oxford became the major shareholder in the circus—about seven or eight months ago—the number of ladies' nights has risen dramatically, to at least five a week.'

'I wonder if that foreshadows anything sinister?' said the Pirate Captain.

'We shouldn't leap to conclusions, just because the unspeakable Bishop is our enemy,' said Darwin reasonably. 'After all, it may be that he feels sorry for ladies, and thinks they could do with some free entertainment.'

'Why would he feel sorry for ladies?' asked the albino pirate.

'Well, what with so many of them going missing lately, and then being found washed up in the River Thames, all shrivelled and lifeless.'

'How long has *that* been going on?'

'Oooh, about seven or eight months, I should say.'

The conversation was interrupted when the pirate with a scarf spotted a policeman coming along the street towards them. The pirates and their companions quickly ducked into Leicester Square.

'It's not safe on the streets for you pirates,' said Darwin, still pushing Mister Bobo along in a pram so as not to draw any unwanted attention. 'Upstairs in the Natural

History Museum there is the Royal Society Gentlemen's Club, where we might plan our course of action.'

'Will they have grog there?' asked the sassy pirate.

'Yes. And cigars. But I don't think they'll let pirates in. And Lord knows what my colleagues would think if they saw me associating with sea dogs like you.'

The pirates were a bit hurt by this, and Darwin was quick to try to save their feelings.

'I mean, obviously, FitzRoy and I know that you're stand-up fellows, it's just the other members . . . they may be rather quick to judge.'

'There's only one thing for it, then,' said the Pirate Captain, a gleam in his eye. 'We'll have to disguise ourselves as scientists!'

Holding pens and rulers, and with white lab coats covering their piratical paraphernalia, the pirates followed Darwin into the Royal Society Gentlemen's Club.* There were several famous scientists present, some sitting around smoking, some engaged in animated discussion about the latest scientific topic, and some just watching the dancing girls. The smell of opium hung heavily in the air.

---

*The Royal Society was set up in 1660, and many famous scientists have been members, including Robert Boyle, Robert Hooke, and John Venn. Why not try drawing a Venn Diagram of 'pirates' (A) and 'ham' (B) and 'barrels of tar' (C)? How large is the intersection (X)?

'Anyhow,' one of the scientists was saying to another, 'there simply isn't room in the museum's Fishes Hall, so we've decided to pretend to the public that a whale is actually a mammal without any legs. It's patently ridiculous—I mean to say, just look at the thing, it's a gigantic fish if ever you saw one—but mum's the word! In my experience the public will believe just about anything, so long as you write it down on a little piece of card.'

The Pirate Captain coughed.

'Goodness! Look, everybody, it's Darwin! Darwin's back!' exclaimed one of the scientists with bushy side-burns, and everybody crowded round Darwin and FitzRoy, slapping them on the shoulders and asking questions. It was a couple of minutes before Darwin could get a word in edgeways.

'Uh, these here are some scientists I met on my travels,' he said, indicating the disguised pirates. 'I hope you'll make them feel welcome.'

'Sorry. We're forgetting our manners. It's just so good to see Charles back, alive and well. One hears such stories about life on the high seas. Giant squids and pirates and the like,' said a genuine scientist, shaking the Pirate Captain's hand. 'What sort of science do you do?'

'What sort of science? Well . . . it's mainly . . . chemicals,' said the Pirate Captain, thinking on his feet. 'There's a lot of stirring things together. And then writing things down, of course.'

'Fascinating,' said the scientist. 'And what about you? What's your field?' he added, turning to the pirate with a hook for his hand.

The pirate with a hook for his hand didn't know what to say, but the quick-witted Pirate Captain cut in deftly. 'My modest colleague does a lot of work with minerals. He likes gold best. He heats it up, with matches.'

'Surely, as a man of science, you'd use a Bunsen burner?'

'Did I say matches? Yes, I meant Bunsen burner. It's been a long day.' The Pirate Captain shrugged apologetically.

The pirates managed to do a pretty decent job of mingling with the scientists, nodding politely and saying 'Really?' a lot as they listened to them drone on about their latest inventions and discoveries, but the Pirate Captain soon found himself involved in a particularly awkward conversation about molecules, so he was relieved when FitzRoy interrupted him before it got to the stage where he had to say if he was for or against them.

'As a fellow nautical man, there's somebody I'd like you to meet,' said FitzRoy, grabbing the Pirate Captain by the sleeve of his lab coat and dragging him over to shake hands with a fresh-faced young scientist.

'This is James Glaisher, the famous meteorologist,' said FitzRoy. The Pirate Captain wasn't sure what a meteorologist did, but he suspected it was something boring.

'James and I have long held the belief that the weather does not operate in some capricious manner, and that with sufficient information, it should be possible to give advance warning of storms at sea. Our voyage has only served to further convince me.'

The Pirate Captain made sure he was doing his best interested-face whilst he wondered what time scientists tended to eat dinner.

'So tell me, James,' continued FitzRoy, 'how have the experiments been going? Did you get a chance to make the modifications I suggested for your ship?'

'What's this?' said the Pirate Captain, his ears pricking up, eager to find a topic he could make head or tail of. 'You have a ship? Why, I have a boat myself!'

'I'm afraid it's not that kind of a ship,' explained the scientist.* 'For some time now, FitzRoy and I have pursued the idea of a motorised weather balloon. I believe it to be the world's first lighter-than-air-ship. A dirigible, if you will.'

'A lighter-than-air-ship?' said the Pirate Captain, rubbing his hairy chin. 'How many cannons does it have? My boat has twelve cannons.'

'Cannons? It doesn't have *any* cannons.'

---

*James Glaisher of the Magnetic and Meteorological Department at the Greenwich Observatory made a series of twenty-nine balloon ascents in the nineteenth century to investigate barometric pressure at altitude.

'You're not going to be much cop when it comes to plundering if you haven't got any cannons!' the Pirate Captain snorted imperiously.

'Plundering? I'm not sure you understand. We've not invented the airship to go plundering.'

'So what on earth *is* it for?' asked the Pirate Captain.

'For? What is all science "for"!' exclaimed the scientist. 'Pushing back frontiers! The thrill of discovery! Advancing the sum total of human knowledge and endeavour! And looking down ladies' tops.'

Over dinner Darwin told the story of his voyage, missing out the bit with the pirates, then he showed off Mister Bobo, who performed impeccably and proved excellent when it came to the after-dinner charades, making everybody laugh as he acted out Daniel Defoe's *Journal of the Plague Year*. All of the scientists agreed that Mister Bobo was a breakthrough, but none of them knew what was to be done about the predicament of Erasmus. A glum gloom settled over the table, and even Darwin's pet bulldog, Huxley, whimpered as it ate the scraps of ham surreptitiously fed to it under the table by the pirate with a scarf.

It was time for action. The Pirate Captain slammed down his After Eight mint with a mighty crash.

'It's clear to me what must be done,' he told the assembled scientists and pirates-dressed-as-scientists. 'Darwin must go ahead and announce a lecture tour with Mister Bobo as if nothing were wrong. I'll get my crew— my scientist crew, that is—to put up posters, and we'll hold the first lecture in this very museum, tomorrow night.'

'But what about the repercussions? Until I know Erasmus is safe, how can I dare?' said Darwin, aghast.

'If my years of experience solving crimes has taught me anything,' said the Pirate Captain, looking reassuringly nonchalant by tipping his chair back dangerously, 'it's that you can't catch a mouse without cheese!'

'Your years of experience solving crimes? But you're a pirate,' whispered Darwin. 'Surely that doesn't involve much detective work?'

'Aarrr,' roared the Pirate Captain, because it seemed a good way to end the conversation.

Eight

BATTLING THE
OCTOPUS!

The next morning, waking up for the first time in three years in a proper bed with fresh linen that didn't stink of fish and monkeys, Darwin felt a great deal better about things. Before he had retired for the night the Pirate Captain had taken him aside and gone on to explain his piratical plan. He reasoned that they had no means of ascertaining the whereabouts of Erasmus until the evil Bishop of Oxford showed his face. By announcing the lecture tour with Mister Bobo they would force the Bishop's hand, and he would be sure to turn up in order to try threatening Darwin into backing down. The Bishop would be expecting scientists. What the Bishop wouldn't be expecting were pirates! At this point the plan got a bit hazy, but Darwin felt confident in the Pirate Captain's abilities nonetheless. He propped himself up on his pillows and flicked through that morning's edition of *The Times,* pretending not to look at the more salacious pictures of table legs. There was another big headline about a mysteriously shrivelled lady being found bobbing about in the Thames, and an article in the Style section where he saw that for the fifth year running, 'sinister and macabre' was still very much in vogue when it came to the Victorian gentleman's interior design choices. He sighed. With sunlight streaming in through the window, and a plate of toast already brought to him by the Royal Society's butler, Darwin was tempted to spend the whole morning in bed, but he had a lot to sort out, so he shook Mister Bobo awake and started preparing for the evening's lecture. A lecture, he pondered, that could make his name as a scientist—and, by that token, hopefully lead to a good deal more success with women.

In one of the Royal Society's bathrooms just down the hall the Pirate Captain was busy flossing.

'Are you going to be in there much longer?' asked an unfamiliar voice with an impatient knock. The Pirate Captain flung open the door, ready to run through with his shiny cutlass whosoever it happened to be, but then he remembered he was supposed to be a mild-mannered scientist, not a bloodthirsty Terror of the High Seas. So instead he fixed the knave who had the cheek to interrupt his toiletries with a steely stare. He recognised one of the scientists from dinner.

'Yes,' growled the Pirate Captain. 'I am going to be in here much longer. Beards like this don't look after themselves, you know.'

'Right, sorry,' said the scientist, backing away meekly. 'Gosh. You've got a lot of scars.'

The Pirate Captain was wearing only a risqué towel, and he did indeed have a number of scars from previous adventures.

'That's from bumping against scientific apparatus in my laboratory,' explained the Pirate Captain, a murderous gleam in his eyes.

'And is that . . . a treasure map tattooed on your belly?'

'No. It's the periodic table.'

'It doesn't look like the periodic table. X isn't an element.'

The Pirate Captain decided to run the scientist through with his cutlass after all. He washed it off in the sink, attended to his beard, and then went back to the room he was sharing with some of the other pirates.

'They may know how to make a mechanical pig,' said the Pirate Captain, 'but these scientists have got a lot to learn about manners.'

The other pirates all nodded at this and sucked thoughtfully on their daily ration of limes, except for the pirate with an accordion, who was sucking on a green Starburst because he didn't much care for proper fruit.

'Now, does everybody know what they're doing today? You two'—the Pirate Captain pointed to the albino pirate and the pirate with a hook where his hand should have been—'will help Mr Darwin with anything he needs for his lecture. And you two'—this time he indicated the scarf-wearing pirate and the pirate with an accordion—'will check out P. T. Barnum's Circus. Why is a Bishop involved in running a circus, that's what I want to know. I'm not sure how it fits in with his diabolical plans, but I have my suspicions about the place. It's ladies' night, so you'll have to disguise yourselves as women.'

'It's going to be quite difficult fitting a lady disguise on top of our scientist disguises, which we're already wearing on top of our pirate outfits,' said the scarf-wearing pirate.

'You'll just have to do your best,' said the Pirate Captain. 'I'd go myself, but obviously my luxuriant beard would make it difficult for me to pass as a lady. And don't forget that ladies speak in squeaky voices. Like this— "Hello, I'm a lady!" '

Everybody laughed at the Pirate Captain's brilliant impression of what a lady sounded like.*

'The rest of you pirates go round town and paste up these posters advertising tonight's lecture.'

---

*Men's vocal cords tend to be thicker than women's, so they produce a deeper tone in exactly the same way that a thick rubber band makes a deeper sound than a thin one when you twang it. You might need to stretch the rubber bands over a biscuit tin to get the full effect.

The Pirate Captain handed out a stack of A4 posters. They were illustrated with a picture of Darwin and Mister Bobo playing chess. Mister Bobo was in Rodin's *The Thinker* pose, and Darwin had thrown his hands up in defeat. The Pirate Captain had drawn the picture himself, and was proud of his effort. Before he became a pirate he was going to be an architect, and he had used his knowledge of perspective and foreshortening to make Mister Bobo's massive monkey behind seem a lot smaller than it was in real life. And he'd managed to give Darwin a genuine look of exasperation at having been bested by a chimp. The only thing about the picture that slightly disappointed the Pirate Captain was Darwin's hands, which looked more like lumpy starfish—for some reason the Pirate Captain had never got very good at drawing hands. Above the picture were the words:

One night only—Mister Charles Darwin will be showing off his fantastic hirsute new friend Mister Bobo—the world's first Man-panzee! Royal Society Lecture Rooms, admission free.

In very small print it was noted that Mister Bobo did not actually play chess to a particularly high standard.

'These are very good, Captain,' said the scarf-wearing pirate, already applying a cherry-coloured lipstick. The Pirate Captain waved away the praise, and mumbled something about how he didn't think it was that good a picture, even though it was obvious how proud he was.

'Now, I hope I can trust you pirates with this. I'm afraid I've got a prior engagement, so I won't be around to help out,' said the Pirate Captain, giving his sternest look to his men, which involved lowering his eyebrows and pursing his lips together.

'What's that, Captain?' asked the accordion-playing pirate, having some difficulty with his bra strap.

'I received a letter this morning, inviting me to attend a Pirate Convention at Earls Court. I'm one of the guests of honour.'

The other pirates occasionally wondered how it was that these letters found their way to their itinerant captain, but somehow they always did.

'A Pirate Convention? You're certain this isn't another of those Royal Navy schemes to trap a whole bunch of pirates?' said the scarf-wearing pirate, his brow furrowed with concern.

'Remember that time they said there was going to be a pirate beauty contest on Mozambique, and we had to shoot our way out?'

'Remember it? Of course I remember it! I still say I was robbed,' pouted the Pirate Captain. His crew nodded—certainly none of them had ever seen another pirate as attractive as their chiselled Captain.

'But, anyhow, the letter came with our secret pirate symbol marked on the envelope. See?' The Pirate Captain pointed to the Jolly Roger* stamped on the seal. 'So it must be the real deal. I'm quite looking forward to it. With any luck I'll be able to sign a few autographs for the kids, and pick up some pirate equipment at bargain prices.'

'All due respects, Captain,' said the pirate in green, feasting on a bowl of cereal, 'but have you really got time to be going off to a Pirate Convention? We're sort of bang in the middle of an adventure here.'

'It's a fair point,' replied the Pirate Captain. 'But I have my reasons. For a start, what with Black Bellamy pulling a fast one on us, the boat's finances aren't looking too healthy, and this could be a chance to make a doubloon or two. Good deeds won't keep us in ham, you know. Secondly, a few of my pirate contacts might come in useful in figuring out just what this Bishop is really up to. And thirdly, I'm the Pirate Captain and I can do whatever the hell I please!'

'Are you planning on wearing that hat to the convention?' asked the pirate in red. The Pirate Captain thought he could detect a certain amount of disapproval in his tone.

'Yes, I am. It happens to be my favourite hat. You may notice that the blue of the trim brings out the blue of my eyes.' The Pirate Captain pointed to the blue trim and then at his blue eyes to emphasise the point.

---

*Though the name 'Jolly Roger' would lead you to expect a picture of a happy-looking man, it is actually a scary skull above two crossed bones.

'Ah. Well, then. I'm sure you know best, Captain.'

'Are you trying to say there's something wrong with my hat?'

'Not at all, Captain. It might not be the most up-to-date choice, but I'm sure there's nothing wrong with that,' said the pirate in red, sounding very much like he thought there was a great deal wrong with it.

'This is a perfectly good pirate hat. It's a tricorn.'

'Exactly.'

'Your point being?'

'It's just . . . nowadays . . . a more Napoleonic design seems to be the choice of the successful pirate. It's generally held to have a touch more . . . *je ne sais quoi*. I'm only saying, is all.'

'My hat has plenty of *je ne sais quoi*. Not to say *joie de vivre*.'

'If you say so.'

'Fine. Hands up, who likes my hat?'

Most of the pirate crew loyally stuck their hands in the air. The pirate in red just shrugged and pretended to be reading a book. Satisfied that the mutinous swab had been put in his place, the Pirate Captain helped himself to another bowl of Cocoa Puffs.

Nine

ENTER THE
PIRATE KING!

B y twelve o'clock the scarf-wearing pirate and the pirate with an accordion were already sweltering under their multiple disguises. You could hardly hear the clanking of their pirate buckles beneath the layers of lab coat and lady's dress each man wore. They didn't know exactly what it was they were meant to be looking for at the sinister circus—the Pirate Captain had simply told them to keep an eye out for anything suspicious. Looking through the glossy circus brochure the pirate with a scarf thought that it all sounded pretty suspicious—a man with no face, a lady with a phobia for tin foil, an out-of-control teen . . . he was worried that they wouldn't know where to start. The queue to get in stretched all the way down the Mall.

'That's a fetching eye patch. Is it just for show?'

It took the pirate with a scarf a few seconds to realise that the question was being directed at him, and by the young lady just ahead of them in the queue. Looking up, he was so taken aback by how pretty she was he almost forgot to answer in a high-pitched voice instead of his normal pirate voice.

'It's . . . that is . . . I've got an astigmatism,' he stuttered. 'The optician says I have to wear the patch until it goes away.'

'You poor thing,' said the girl, with a look of real concern. 'Would you like a sandwich? It's Serrano ham.'

The pirate with a scarf gratefully took the proffered sandwich. He thought he had better make introductions. 'Thank you. I'm . . . Francine. And this is, erm, Daphne,' he said.

'Jennifer. That's a very shiny accordion you have there, Daphne.'

The pirate with an accordion just grunted, because his lady voice wasn't particularly realistic.

'You're extremely rugged. For a girl,' said Jennifer, turning back to the pirate with a scarf.

'Thank you,' said the pirate, unconsciously flexing the muscles in his back, and knitting his eyebrows together in what he hoped was a suave manner.

'Are you here to see the Mermaid?' asked Jennifer. 'I've heard it's a bit disappointing. Just the top half of a monkey stitched to the bottom half of a fish.'

'Erm, no. That is, not in particular.'

'The albino then?'

'Actually, one of our friends is an albino,' said the pirate brightly.

'Ooh! Is it true that if you ever look directly into their eyes, you turn into an albino yourself? And that they can only eat white things, like vanilla ice cream and milky bars?'

'I don't think so. I'm not entirely sure.'

'I wonder if they can eat mallow?'

Jennifer seemed to be lost in her deliberations about albinos. If the pirate with a scarf had been more poetically minded he'd have thought that her eyes were like a thousand emeralds, glittering in a far-off pirate treasure chest. But he wasn't, so he just thought that she had really *really* green eyes, a bit like seaweed.

'What about you? What are you here to see?' asked the pirate quickly, anxious to keep the conversation going. 'The Elephant Man?'

'Not really. Between you and me'—at this point Jennifer put her mouth alarmingly close to the pirate with a scarf's ear—'I think something sinister is going on at the circus. My sister Beatrice visited it last week, and that's the last we ever saw of her.'

'I think you could be right,' said the pirate, completely forgetting the undercover nature of their mission because of the shape of her neck. 'In fact, we're here to investigate. I'm not even really a lady.'

The pirate with a scarf briefly raised his dress.

'You're a scientist!'

The pirate remembered to lift up his lab coat as well.

'You're a pirate!'

'Yes, but don't tell anybody.'

Half an hour later Jennifer and the two pirates were through the turnstiles and inside the circus itself. The pirate with an accordion pretty quickly started to feel more like the pirate who was a gooseberry, so he wandered off to look at an exhibit that claimed to be 'the dog that wore sunglasses', and left Jennifer and the scarf-wearing pirate to their own devices. The circus was sprawled across St James's Park, and a blanket of thick London fog hung between the various tents. The pair decided to start their investigations with the Elephant Man. He was sitting in the centre of a little hut looking a bit forlorn, whilst a man with a tuba played a few bars of 'Nellie the Elephant' over and over again.

'He doesn't look big enough to have eaten my sister,' said Jennifer. 'But he might know something.'

'We should try to gain his confidence by carrying on a pleasant conversation,' whispered the pirate.

'I'll have a go,' nodded Jennifer. She took a few steps towards the creature and cleared her throat.

'Wow!' she said. 'So you're the Elephant Man! That's some face!'

It wasn't exactly the opening gambit the pirate with a

scarf had in mind, but he bit his lip because the closest he had come recently to having any success with a girl was the time a few weeks before when he had drunk too much rum, and ended up thinking he was in love with the pirate boat's figurehead. The boat's figurehead was certainly attractive, and extremely well carved, but it left him with nasty splinters whenever he tried to give it a hug.

'I'd—uh—prefer it if you called me John,' said the Elephant Man, trying to crack a smile. 'My name is John Merrick.'

'Okay, John it is. So let me get this straight . . . you got turned into an elephant-*man* by being bitten by an actual elephant, is that right? Was the elephant radioactive in any way?' asked Jennifer.

'Ah . . . no. I suffer from a rare genetic condition. It causes the rapid growth of bony tumours. There are no elephants involved. Several unfortunate children are born with it every year.'

'Children are born with it? Is that because their mothers have been bitten by an elephant whilst pregnant? Are you saying that if I got pregnant, I shouldn't visit a zoo?'

'No. Really, the condition has nothing to do with elephants.'

'Would the baby only be affected if the mother was bitten in the belly by an elephant? Or would a bite to the leg do it too?'

'I don't think you're really listening . . . ,' said the Elephant Man with as much patience as he could muster.

'I can tell you're from India, because of the shape of your ears,' added Jennifer triumphantly. The Elephant Man just sighed and shook his head.

'Tell me, John,' Jennifer went on, swiftly changing tack. 'Do you know why this circus has so many ladies' nights? I mean, they're virtually every night! It's suspicious!'

'No. No, I don't. I . . . I don't even know what you're talking about,' said the Elephant Man quickly. The pirate with a scarf thought he saw a flash of fear in the wretch's eyes, but it was hard to tell because his face was such a funny shape.

'Listen. Why don't I sing you a song?' said the Elephant Man, obviously desperate to try to change the subject. He even got up and did a little ungainly jig as he sang.

I look like some ex-pe-ri-ment!
But please believe me I'm a proper gent!
I seem like a monster, but whatcha don't know is,
*I got a scorching case of neurofibromatosis!**

*Or possibly Proteus Syndrome. There is still some debate in medical circles. Contrary to popular belief, Michael Jackson never did purchase the Elephant Man's skeleton from the Royal Hospital. This is a good example of how you shouldn't believe everything that people tell you.

Jennifer and the pirate with a scarf gave up on getting a straight answer, and went to search for any clues that might be evident at the other exhibits. But they had no more luck with the Man Who Could Eat a Bicycle, or the Lady Who Had Had Hiccups for Forty Years, or even with the Girl from Chesterfield Who Would Repeatedly Go Out with Idiots When She Could Do a Great Deal Better for Herself. The pea-soup fog was starting to make their eyes sting, so Jennifer and the pirate ducked inside a tent that was simply marked 'A Special Exhibit for the Ladies'. It didn't seem very special—it was just an empty and badly lit tent as far as the pirate with a scarf could make out.

'It's very dark in here. I can't even see what we're meant to be looking at,' said Jennifer, slipping her hand through her companion's arm. The pirate with a scarf's heart skipped a beat. He couldn't believe how well it was going. Usually by this point with a girl he'd have said something idiotic, or spilt drink all down his front, or chewed with his mouth open, but he'd managed not to do any of those things so far, and he even seemed to be impressing her with some of his nautical anecdotes.

'It must mean a good deal of responsibility, being the first mate on a pirate boat,' said Jennifer, shivering at a sudden breeze that seemed to blow through the tent.

'It's not easy. But I try to look after my crew,' said the pirate. 'I saved a man's life the other day. He got attacked by a huge jellyfish, and I neutralised the sting by pouring a bucket of wee all over him.'

He instantly wished he had instead told her about the time he fought a monstrous manatee, because it cast him in a slightly more heroic light, and didn't involve big buckets of wee. Jennifer had gone very quiet, and looking up from his shoes—he was terrible at making eye contact with girls he liked—the pirate with a scarf was surprised to see her slumping unconscious to the floor. For one frightened moment he thought his conversation might have sent her into a daze, so he was pretty relieved when he felt a chloroform-soaked rag press against his mouth, and blacked out himself.

The pirate with a scarf opened his eyes groggily. His vision seemed to go cloudy, but then he realised it was just his breath condensing on the inside of the massive glass tube in which he now found himself trapped. The tube was attached to some kind of improbable contraption, fashioned of wood and brass and covered in cogs, pipes, and hissing gaskets. Looking to his left, he saw that Jennifer was held in an identical predicament. With a sinking feeling, he realised that yet again a date with a pretty girl had gone horribly wrong. He could just make out that they were in some kind of big square room, with what looked like gigantic stained-glass windows for walls. He gave a peevish sigh—he certainly wasn't enjoying this adventure as much as, say, the Pirates' Adventure on the Island of Rum and Amazons.

'So, young scarf-wearing lady! You and your pretty friend are awake!'

The room was so dingy, and so cluttered with menacing-looking bric-a-brac, that the pirate hadn't noticed a figure dressed all in black robes* busying about in the corner. It was the iniquitous Bishop of Oxford himself! The pirate with a scarf could tell it was the Bishop because he was wearing a bishop's hat, just like the chess pieces that he had seen the Pirate Captain play with on occasion. The pirate with a scarf preferred Ludo or Snakes and Ladders himself.

'What's all this about, you beast?' asked Jennifer from inside her big glass tube. The Bishop fixed her with a beady stare.

'How old would you take me for?' he asked, as if by way of explanation. Jennifer had never been particularly good at estimating this sort of thing, but she hazarded a guess anyhow.

'Mid-to-late forties?'

'Hah! I'm actually fifty-one years old.'

The Bishop gazed at the pair of them expectantly. Jen-

---

*Black looks best on persons who have black in their features (hair, eyes, brows, and lashes), although black can be worn by most people for very dramatic occasions.

nifer and the pirate with a scarf just looked blankly back at him. He seemed a bit annoyed that he had to explain things further.

'I keep myself so fresh looking by using this devilish machine to distil the very life-essence from young ladies such as you!' he added impatiently.

'So *you're* responsible for all these grisly murders! I had my bets on it being a member of the Royal Family. Or maybe gypsies,' said Jennifer, wide-eyed and fuming. 'You villain!'

'I must say, Bishop,' said the pirate with a scarf— remembering to keep up his lady voice—'the sack and the drugs. It's not the sort of behaviour I'd expect from a man of the cloth.'

The diabolical Bishop looked almost sheepish.

'I realise that my methods leave a lot to be desired,' he replied with a rather forlorn sigh, 'but you have to appreciate the climate I'm working in. Anyone will tell you how difficult it is to meet a nice girl in a big city like this. So you can understand that in my case, where I need to meet about a dozen nice girls a week in order to synthesise my ghastly concoction . . . well, it's virtually impossible.'

'I can see why you're not a girl's first choice,' said Jennifer with a sneer. 'If a lady is looking for anything to be planted on her mouth at the end of an evening, it's a kiss, not a dirty old cloth soaked in chloroform. The least I'd expect of a fellow who intends to drain the youthful life-force out of me would be flowers and conversation.'

'Yes, it's a bit much. Do you really need the sinister circus and the swirling fog and the kidnapping? Have you tried a nice coffee shop? I hear that they're great places to pick up us women,' said the pirate helpfully.

'Of course I have!' replied the Bishop with an air of despair. 'But it just never works out. I meet a girl, I laugh a booming maniacal laugh at their anecdotes, just like I've read you're meant to, and I make sure to pay them a compliment—"You've got a lovely hairline, I won't need to shave your temples when I attach you to my nightmarish device"—something like that. But more often than not it's a swift peck on the cheek, thanks for a lovely evening, and I'm home alone in my macabre lair. I just don't have time for it! I'm not getting any younger, you know. Well, I suppose in a manner of speaking I am, but you see my point.'

'I doubt that funny little moustache is doing you any favours,' said Jennifer with an arched eyebrow.

'It's an evil moustache, not a gay moustache,' replied the Bishop with a pout.

'That's why you're so bothered by Darwin's Manpanzee!' exclaimed the pirate. 'You're worried that if Mister Bobo is a roaring success, then all the crowds will forget about the Elephant Man, and they'll flock to see him instead! Without a constant supply of young ladies visiting the circus for you to kidnap, you wouldn't be able to fashion your evil elixir!'

'It's not really an elixir. It's more a sort of facial

scrub,'* said the Bishop. 'But listen, I'm not about to let you gab your way out of this. On with the show!'

The Bishop threw an enormous lever, and his horrific machine roared into life. Sparks bounced off the walls, pistons smashed up and down, lights flashed, and bells rang. But just as the contraption seemed to be building to a crescendo there was a sickening metallic gurgle, a belch of acrid black smoke, and everything fell silent.

'Oh, for pity's sake!' moaned the Bishop, giving an apologetic look to his captives. 'Honestly, this has never happened before.' He spent the next few minutes trying fruitlessly to find a fault with the various gears and pulleys and bits of wire that made up his machine. The pirate with a scarf took this opportunity to attempt a bit of romantic small talk with Jennifer, but she seemed a little preoccupied and he could sense that the moment might have passed.

'There's no reason why this shouldn't be working. It's brand new,' said the Bishop tetchily. 'Unless . . . one of you isn't really a lady!'

The pirate with a scarf gulped, and tried to do his most winning lady smile, but then he realised that this just showed off more of his gold teeth.

---

*The Bishop of Oxford was widely known as 'Soapy' Sam Wilberforce. However, if you look this up on Google, chances are it will ascribe the nickname to his 'slippery ecclesiastical debating skills' rather than his habit of turning ladies into bars of soap.

'There's only one way to find out,' said the Bishop, a nasty reptilian grin playing across his face as he advanced upon Jennifer and the disguised pirate.

Forty minutes later, the two of them reluctantly handed the Bishop their completed psychometric test papers. He pored over the results, and then pointed an accusing finger at the pirate. The scarf-wearing pirate hung his head in dismay—his skill at spatial awareness and numerical pattern identification compared with his comparative weakness at colour differentiation and verbal reasoning had given away his secret.

'You're no lady!' said the Bishop with a scowl. 'In fact, these test results suggest you're a pirate! Goodness knows what you've done to my machine. It's only designed to work with ladies aged nineteen to twenty-six. You've probably invalidated my warranty, you lousy bum.'

The Bishop unhooked the pirate from his infernal apparatus, and rolled him in his tube over to what looked for all the world like a massive metal cog. Then he opened up the top of the tube, slid the bound pirate out, and fastened him to one of the notches between the cog's gigantic teeth. The Bishop looked at his watch irritably. 'I've got an appointment with a man and his monkey,' he said, turning his attention to Jennifer. 'But I expect you to be a lifeless husk by the time I get back, young lady. No funny business.'

With that, he pulled the big lever again, and went off whistling a show tune. The pirate with a scarf looked on in horror as the life started to drain from what was the first girl in ages who looked as though she might actually have put out for him.

Ten

A DEAD MAN'S CHEST!

Halfway across town the Pirate Captain strode along with big piratical strides. He didn't stare down at his feet and scuttle through the sudden downpour like the sorry rubbernecks who shared the narrow streets with him; he held his head high and seemed almost to be snarling at the sky, willing it to do its worst—he was the Pirate Captain, and he wasn't bothered by a bit of rain.

Just a few minutes later—he walked at quite a pace, and had been known to swing his cutlass at ditherers who blocked his way—the Pirate Captain arrived at the Hotel Metropolitan, where, according to his letter, the Pirate

Convention was being held. The concierge, a slight and sweaty man, greeted him in the swanky lobby.

'You must be here for the Pork Convention,' he said with an exaggerated wink.

'Pork Convention? Are you mad? I'm here for the Pirate Convention!' said the Pirate Captain, dumbfounded.

'Ha-ha! A Pirate Convention!' laughed the concierge, nervously brushing some of his few remaining hairs across a shiny scalp. 'Imagine! If you were an otherwise respectable hotel, and you were to hold a Pirate Convention, why'—the concierge gave a meaningful pause—'you'd probably pretend it was a Pork Convention, or something like that.'

'What's this blathering about pork?'

'I think that's what you're looking for.'

'I'm looking for no such thing! And stop winking at me! I've run men through for less!'

'I was simply saying the word "pork" instead of "pirate" so as not to draw any unwanted attention to the proceedings. It's a kind of clever code. It doesn't really matter anymore,' whispered the concierge, a touch irritably.

'Ah! Yes. I'm here for the Pork Convention,' said the Pirate Captain in a loud voice, adding quietly with a wink of his own, 'I see what you're doing now.'

'If you'll just follow me.'

'Certainly. Is there anywhere I can leave my gammon?'

'I'm sorry?'

'My gammon. It's clever code for "cutlass". I just made it up.'

The concierge led the Pirate Captain through the lobby, which had been smartly decked out with big misleading papier-mâché models of different kinds of pork products—including chops and sausages—across an expensive-looking carpet, and into the hotel's main conference hall. It was full to the brim with pirates from all over the globe. Several of them were roaring, so it was quite noisy, and there was a distinct smell of seaweed about the place. Scanning the room, which read like a *Who's Who* of the nautical underworld, the Pirate Captain recognised a familiar figure. He threaded his way through the crowd.

'Raagh! You lubber!' roared the Pirate Captain.

'What's that? Lubber! Who's calling me a lubber! You cur!' said the pirate, spinning round angrily. He must have been a good seven feet tall, with hands the size of the hams the Pirate Captain usually ate for dinner. Several of the other pirates in the immediate vicinity fell silent, their hands on their cutlasses, expecting trouble. But the giant pirate held up his arms and proceeded to squeeze the Pirate Captain in an embrace that would have crushed the breath out of lesser men with a more limited lung capacity.

'Why! It's my old friend the Pirate Captain!' bellowed the pirate.

'Scurvy Jake!' said the Pirate Captain, evidently glad to

see his former comrade. 'I haven't seen you since that incident on Madagascar!'

'Aaarrr! I was sure they were girls!' said Scurvy Jake with an apologetic shrug.

'What are you doing here, you salty old dog?' laughed the Pirate Captain, giving his friend an affectionate slap on his oversized biceps.

'I'm in the nostalgia business!' said Scurvy Jake, indicating the convention buzzing on around them. 'I mean, after I hung up my eye patch I tried my hand at a few things, but what with the Industrial Revolution, it's all factory work. I'm not cut out for all that fiddly business, haven't got the fingers for it.' Scurvy Jake indicated his fingers, which were the size of bananas.* 'But then I found out how lucrative going on the Pirate Convention circuit can be. You sign a few books, tell a couple of stories, there's plenty of grog in return, and you get free board and lodging to boot. I'm actually a lot better at reminiscing about pirating than I ever was at doing it in the first place.'

Scurvy Jake helped the Pirate Captain to a complimentary glass of rum.†

---

*Edible bananas may disappear within a decade if urgent action is not taken to develop new varieties resistant to blight, according to recent studies published in *New Scientist*.
†Rum is the oldest distilled spirit in the world. After he was killed at the Battle of Trafalgar, Lord Nelson's body was preserved in a barrel of his favourite rum. To make a good Mai Tai, you need 1 oz. Dark Rum, 1 oz. Light Rum, 1 oz. Triple Sec, $^1/_2$ oz. Lime Juice, $^1/_2$ oz. Grenadine, $^1/_2$ oz. Orgeat Syrup. Garnish with a pineapple wedge and cherry. Serve in a High Ball.

'Let me show you the ropes,' the giant continued. 'There's a panel quiz later on where fans can ask us a few questions, and everybody tends to hit the bar after that. But right now I'm going to sign a few photos of myself. I charge a doubloon a time. Care to join me?'

As it happened the Pirate Captain had stopped off at a Victorian Snappy Snaps, and was clutching a stack of black-and-white six-by-eights, in which he was doing a very debonair face indeed. He settled down at a table next to Scurvy Jake and pretty soon had a queue of asthmatic-looking kids and creepy middle-aged men lining up in front of him. He'd been sort of hoping that groupies might prove to be a problem—girls who wanted nothing more than to annoy their respectable families by throwing themselves at a handsome Pirate Captain—but it was immediately obvious that they were going to be in short supply.

'Could you sign it to Paul,' said the first fan to come shambling up. 'And maybe put something like "Arrgh! Here be treasure!" I was going to stick it on top of my money box, you see.'

'Certainly. That's very clever.'

'My money box is shaped like a pirate boat.'

'Even better,' said the Pirate Captain, handing him his picture with a grin.

'You're fantastic!' said another eager young boy.

'Ah, I don't know if I'd go that far . . .'

'No, really, you are. I was even going to buy a resin model of you swinging on some rigging, but I only had six shillings, so I got Black Bellamy instead. Have you ever met Black Bellamy? He's my favourite pirate ever!'

'Is that a fact?'

'Oh yes. He's terrific. You're almost as good, though. But why are you wearing a hat like that?'

'This happens to be a very stylish pirate hat.'

'Black Bellamy has some brilliant hats. You should talk to him to find out where he gets his hats from.'

'How would you like to be run through by a genuine pirate cutlass?'

Ker-chunk!

Back in the Bishop's gloomy lair the pirate with a scarf was starting to realise the nature of his predicament. Every few minutes the massive cog to which he was tied clicked on a few inches. It meshed with another gigantic cog, and he estimated that in a couple of hours he would reach this second set of metallic teeth and be crushed to a pulp of bone and gristle and bits of scarf. The only consolation was that he had found Erasmus Darwin, who was tied between two teeth a little further round, and would be crushed to death several minutes before him. And as the Bishop's monstrous contraption continued to chug away, Jennifer would probably be worse off even sooner. Neither fact was actually much consolation at all.

'Are you okay?' said the pirate to Jennifer.

'My fingertips have started to shrivel up a bit. It's like I've been in the bath too long.'*

'Listen. Assuming we get out of this, how would you like to come out to dinner with me?' The pirate gave what he imagined to be a sexy wink.

'Oh. Well ... I've sort of got plans,' said Jennifer. Erasmus made a sound like a plane crashing. The pirate with a scarf shot him a bit of a look, and started to wonder why he had bothered getting out of his hammock that morning.

Just then there came the wheezy sound of an accordion. It was an odd little tune that, had he been alive exactly one hundred and fifty years later, the scarf-wearing pirate would have recognised as the first few bars from 'Theme to *Murder, She Wrote*'. Out from behind a gigantic bell stepped the pirate with an accordion. The others were unanimously glad to see him.

'Rescue!' cried Erasmus.

'Daphne!' said Jennifer.

'What took you so long?' asked the pirate with a scarf, in a bit of a strop.

'You two wandered off, so I went to the hall of mirrors,' said the pirate with an accordion defensively. 'It

---

*There's no need to be frightened when your fingers shrivel up after being in the bath. Normally your skin is lubricated with a thin layer of sebum—an oil which acts to waterproof the surface of your body. With prolonged exposure to water the sebum is washed away, which allows water to penetrate into the epidermis by osmosis. The skin becomes waterlogged, resulting in a wrinkled appearance—rather like a monster or an old woman.

was fantastic! One of the mirrors made me look like a little dwarf, but with a big long head! I laughed for ages! And then I got bored of that, so I played a bit of "What shall we do with the drunken sailor?" on my accordion, which happens to be my favourite shanty. Then I tried to find you and your girlfriend.'

'She's not my girlfriend,' said the scarf-wearing pirate with a scowl.

'Bad luck. Anyhow, I noticed the pair of you going into that Special Exhibit for the Ladies, and when you didn't come out for ages I thought perhaps you were teaching Jennifer about tying knots.'

'Knots?'

'You must have noticed how whenever there's a lady on board the pirate boat, the Pirate Captain will always disappear into his cabin with her for a while, and afterwards, when any of us ask what they were doing, he tells us he was just teaching the lady how to tie knots, because most girls don't know much about nautical matters. Between you and me, I think he must tell funny anecdotes at the same time as showing them how to tie knots, because quite often I've heard a lot of giggling. But that's not to say the Captain doesn't take his knot tying seriously—he obviously puts a lot of effort into it, as he tends to come out from a knot-tying lesson looking quite exhausted.'

The pirate with a scarf wondered if it were perhaps time to sit down with some of the crew and set them straight on a couple of matters.

'So eventually I decided to follow you into the tent myself,' continued the pirate with an accordion. 'But you were nowhere to be seen! It was completely empty, except for a half-used-up bottle of chloroform. I looked about for a while, and then I found there was a trapdoor hidden in the floor, which led to some steps. And the steps led to a creepy-looking tunnel. Well, that all seemed rather rum. I think it was part of an old sewer system, and you know how you're always reading about people flushing away baby alligators which then grow to gigantic proportions, so—given that alligators and us pirates have got a bit of a troubled history—I was pretty frightened, but I played the most upbeat shanties I could think of to keep myself calm. The tunnel went on for a few hundred yards, and then I got to more stairs, lots of them this time, and they led up here. Now I've found you I suppose I should probably—'

But without saying another word, the pirate with an accordion died of scurvy, right there and then.

'Blast,' said Erasmus.

'I wasn't expecting that,' said Jennifer miserably.

'Idiot!' said the pirate with a scarf. 'I told him what would happen if he just ate candy all the time instead of limes.'

Scurvy Jake and the Pirate Captain had gone on signing autographs for most of the afternoon. Occasionally the Pirate Captain got a bit annoyed to hear Scurvy Jake passing off one of the Pirate Captain's exciting anecdotes as if it were his own, but he decided to let it slide. After they had both run out of photographs—the Pirate Captain was pleased to have pocketed over sixty doubloons for his efforts—they decided to wander over to the part of the convention where several stalls were selling piratical equipment at trade prices. There was a lot of good-natured bargaining going on, as pirates jostled each other for the best deals. The Pirate Captain picked up a job lot of thirty portholes for just twenty-eight pounds—less than a pound per porthole! He also bought a barrel of tar, six bottles of Pirate Rum, and a few tricorn hats just to spite everybody. Satisfied with his purchases, he and Scurvy Jake headed over to the Metropolitan's bar to drink and reminisce.

Pretty soon Scurvy Jake was a bit worse the wear from all the grog.

'I was a terrible pirate,' he said in a cracked voice. 'You were always a much better pirate than me.'

It was true, thought the Pirate Captain. Scurvy Jake had always been a rubbish pirate. With his lumbering lack of coordination and his giant hands, he was no good at tying knots, and he was famous for repeatedly burying treasure and then forgetting where he'd left it. But the Pirate Captain didn't like to see his old friend upset.

'Pfft! I've made a few mistakes myself,' said the Pirate Captain, trying to console him. 'Like that time I let a cannibal join the crew. And that other time when I said, "Well, I don't see any hurricane." I'm not perfect.'

'But I'm the worst pirate ever. I'm so clumsy,' sobbed Scurvy Jake.

'What about Courteous Frank? He was easily a worse pirate than you ever were. I heard he refused to let his crew cure the ship's meat with salt, because he'd read that a high sodium intake had been linked to heart disease. Died eating a slice of rancid ham. You're not even close!'

'It's kind of you to say so, Pirate Captain. You know, if there's anything I can do to help, you just have to ask. Are you on holiday, or are you on an adventure?'

'Adventure. And you can help, Scurvy Jake!' The Pirate Captain's beard glittered with piratical cunning. 'Do you know where I could get hold of a big white sheet?'

Eleven

MAROONED!

'He's not just evil! He's insane! A one hundred per cent Grade-A lunatic!' shouted Darwin, flinging the evening edition of the *Mail* at the Pirate Captain, who had returned from his Pirate Convention and was helping set up the stage of the Natural History Museum's lecture room for the evening's performance. 'The Bishop of Oxford has persisted with his ridiculous scare-mongering. Now he's saying that if I go ahead with my Man-panzee demonstration, the Holy Ghost—the Holy Ghost!—will personally make an appearance at my lecture, and wrestle me and Mister Bobo to the ground! Really, it's too much!'

'It's not the Bishop's work. It's mine,' said the Pirate Captain, chewing the end off a fat cigar, and looking smug. Sometimes the Pirate Captain found himself thinking what a fantastic, hard-bitten, and wily newspaper mogul he would have made, had he not taken up piracy instead. Darwin slumped into one of the auditorium's seats.

'I'm not sure I follow,' he said weakly.

'I'm the one who started the rumour. And—even though I say it myself—it's a stroke of genius.'

'For pity's sake, why?'

'Listen, Charles. You've got a lot to learn about this science business. It's not all about test tubes and creatures and bits of gauze.'

'It isn't?'

'No, it isn't. The whole thing became clear to me when I was talking to an old friend of mine. He was telling me how great at pirating he always thought I was,' explained the Pirate Captain. 'And the fact is, I have made something of a name for myself in nautical circles. But why do you think that is?'

Darwin scratched his head thoughtfully. 'Your luxuriant beard?'

'Aaarrr,' said the Pirate Captain. 'That probably plays a part in it. But more than that, I think it's because of my gift for showmanship. Like the way I drink rum mixed with gunpowder, even though it tastes disgusting. And the way I run people through in such a grisly manner.'

'Surely,' said Darwin, 'it's not possible to be run through in any manner other than a grisly one?'

'Now, a lot of people will tell you that. But it's not the

case. You take the pirate with a scarf. He's such a profi-
cient swordsman that I've seen him run a man through
without spilling a drop of blood,* and the fellow on the
receiving end dies in a speedy and humane fashion. Me,
on the other hand, I'm forever making a mess of it,
hacking about all over the shop, getting my cutlass stuck
in a particularly tough bit of gristle. Yet, quite inadver-
tently, this has all added to my fearsome reputation! And
with pirating, reputation is everything.'

'I'm *still* not sure I follow you,' said the puzzled young
scientist.

'Mister Bobo is a fantastic achievement. But there's a
thousand other scientists out there trying to make a
name for themselves. So if you're going to stand out and
impress the stony-faced Victorian establishment, you
need a gimmick! A bit of controversy! It's all about the
presentation.'

So the Pirate Captain explained his latest plan.
Though perhaps it was a little more complicated than his
usual plans, which tended to involve how much ham to
eat, the Pirate Captain was confident of success. Darwin
was less certain.

'I don't know, Pirate Captain,' he said with a sad shake
of his head, once the Captain had finished. 'It all seems

---

*There are roughly eight pints of blood in the average human. Blood contains red cells,
white cells, and platelets suspended in a proteinacious fluid called plasma. The first
dog biscuit to be made entirely out of blood was invented by Tamsin Virgo, a young
woman from Stoke, England.

such a risk. This lecture is expressly against the Bishop's wishes. I can't help but think something truly terrible will befall my poor brother.'

'Well, I'm in the same boat myself,' said the Pirate Captain with a shrug. 'Two of my pirates never returned from investigating that sinister circus. There's a good chance the Bishop has some evil fate planned for them too. I'm not really that bothered about the swab with the accordion, but that other fellow . . . the one with a scarf'—the Pirate Captain really never seemed to be able to remember the names of any of his crew—'the truth is, I'm at a bit of a loss without him. He cleans my hats, keeps me up-to-date with all the latest shanties, and he even knows all the proper nautical terms for things. I bet you didn't realise that on a sailing boat you're not even meant to say "upstairs" or "downstairs" or "left" or "right". It's all "port" this and "starboard" that and "galley" instead of kitchen and goodness knows what else. How am I expected to remember that kind of thing? Anyhow. What was the point I was making?'

'I'm not really sure,' said Darwin.

'Well then,' said the Pirate Captain, flashing the scientist his most winning grin.

The Royal Society's grandfather clock struck a quarter past ten. It was just a few minutes to go until Darwin's big moment, and the lecture hall was fast filling up. Most of the audience had read the evening papers' controversial headlines, and there was an excited buzz of anticipation throughout the room. The Pirate Captain's ploy had certainly done the trick in bringing in the crowds, thought Darwin. He stood at the door, greeting people as they arrived, whilst Mister Bobo paced backstage taking nervous swigs from a flask of whisky.

'Nice that you could make it. Hi. Hello. Thanks for coming. Glad you could be here. Nice to—'

Darwin froze. He found himself face to face with the Bishop of Oxford.

'Darwin.'

'Bishop.'

'So you're going ahead with this?'

'I—uh—that is . . . it looks that way.'

'What a pity your brother Erasmus couldn't be here.'

'You villain! What have you done with him?'

'Mr Darwin . . . Charles. I haven't the slightest clue what you're talking about. I just hope his health isn't suffering,' said the Bishop, waggling his bushy brows and grimacing to show that he meant the exact opposite of what he was saying. 'It's not too late to reconsider,' he added as he took his seat in the audience, unwittingly right next to the Pirate Captain, who was back in scientist disguise.

The lights dimmed, the thick velvet curtain went up, and Darwin and Mister Bobo came out to enormous applause.

'Ladies and gentlemen. He's hairy! He's scary! I would like to introduce you to the world's first fantastic . . . Man-panzee!'

The spotlight fell on Mister Bobo, who was so well turned out, with his hair slicked back, a breath mint in his mouth, and his best dress shirt tucked into a pair of handsome trousers, that it looked like he was going on a first date. In actual fact, Mister Bobo had never so much as kissed a girl. The audience clapped again. Darwin coughed nervously, and started to explain how he fed Mister Bobo on a diet of pituitary glands taken from the cadavers of baby seals.

'One might expect the pituitary gland to have some effect on the language capabilities of the simian brain, but I can't detect any. Mister Bobo just seems to like the taste,' said Darwin.

Ker-chunk!

The gigantic cog clicked on another notch.

'Shall we have a game of animal, vegetable, or mineral? To take our minds off things?' suggested Erasmus brightly. The scarf-wearing pirate would have enjoyed a game of hangman more, but seeing as they didn't have any chalk, and their hands were all tied up anyhow, he nodded reluctantly.

'I'll go first,' said the pirate. 'Okay, I've thought of something.'

'Are you a mineral?' asked Erasmus.

'Nope.'

'Animal?'

'Sort of.'

'Sort of?'

'All right, yes. Animal.'

'Are you a hoofed animal?'

'No.'

'Claws?'

'No.'

'Not claws or hoofs? What does that leave? Trotters?'

'Yes!'

'So you're a pig?'

'Not exactly . . .'

'Not exactly a pig? Then a bit of a pig? Are you bacon?'

'No, but you're getting warm.'

'Ham?'

'That's it! I'm a succulent piece of ham! But you took too many guesses, so I won, and I get to choose again.'

Darwin had finished his introduction and explanation of his training methods, and now he was leading Mister Bobo—who was doing his best not to knuckle-walk, because he knew just how vulgar that looked—over to a carefully laid out dinner table in the centre of the stage.

'Mister Bobo—would you be so kind as to show these ladies and gentlemen exactly which of these spoons you would use to eat a dessert?'

Mister Bobo held up the correct spoon almost instantly, and the audience let out some 'oohs' and 'aahs'. His confidence building, Mister Bobo proceeded to run through the rest of the routine with aplomb. Shown pictures of two different girls, he correctly identified which one was more attractive, he made a selection of cocktails called out by the audience, and he played 'God Save the Queen' and 'Crockett's Theme' on the piano, without hitting a single wrong note.

Ker-chunk!

'So you're not actually a cow?' said Jennifer, rolling her eyes in exasperation.

'No,' grinned the pirate with a scarf.

'Are you a steak?'

'No!'

'I give up.'

'I'm a sausage! But one made out of beef instead of pork. Right—I've thought of something else!'

'Is this going to be meat-based again?'

'It might be.'

Darwin and Mister Bobo were building up to the grand finale. The lecture had gone well, and the audience seemed politely impressed, but it clearly needed something more to whip them into a frenzy. With a pre-arranged signal from Mister Bobo, a clattering noise came from offstage, and then a lumbering figure appeared.

'Wait a minute! Who's this?' said Darwin, looking surprised. 'Oh my goodness! Ladies and Gentlemen . . . it's the Holy Ghost!'

'Wooo! Raaah!' said the Holy Ghost, a bit muffled, sounding a lot like Scurvy Jake with a sheet over his head. There was the plink-plink of gentlemen dropping monocles into their drinks and the gentle rustle of several ladies fainting.

'He's come to get me, because my theories are so blasphemous!' shouted Darwin, in mock terror. Nobody noticed the twinkle in his eye. 'The Holy Ghost is attacking me! Look at the Holy Ghost!'

'Rah!' said the Holy Ghost, in a booming voice. 'The science you are doing is too shocking by half! I've come to wrestle you! I will lay the smackdown on your wicked ways!'

Gasps shot round the auditorium, and Darwin was pleased to see he had the audience on the edge of their seats. He just had time to notice the Pirate Captain lean over to the Bishop and whisper something in his ear, before his attention was diverted by the Holy Ghost picking him up and hurling the young scientist straight through the middle of the dining table.*

'Dear me! The actual Holy Ghost!' the Pirate Captain was saying to his neighbour. 'If I'd done any sins, I'd probably want to get them off my chest right about now. Like that time I kidnapped somebody. I'm really sorry about that. What about you, Bishop? Have you ever done any sins? Like kidnapping?'

'That's not the Holy Ghost,' snorted the Bishop dismissively.

'Yes it is!' said the Pirate Captain, a bit put out. 'Look how tall he is! He's a giant! And he's covered in a big sheet! Just like it describes him in the Bible.'

'The Bible says nothing of the kind. Where on earth did you get the idea that the Holy Ghost is a giant? He's the same size as Jesus. That's the point—he's just a creepier version of Christ.'

'Are you sure?' frowned the Captain, wondering if his research had let him down. 'Doesn't he fight Goliath at some point? I'm sure he does. He throws a leper at his face.'

---

*Wrestlers today are highly trained professionals, and obviously you should never try smacking people about the head with chairs or throwing them through tables at home. Even the best wrestlers get injured—Mick Foley, three times WWF champion, has broken most of the bones in his body during his career, lost several teeth and even an ear.

'No. I've no idea where you've picked all this up from.'

'It's just after the bit where he hides in that gigantic wooden horse. Isn't it?'

'I think you're a trifle confused.'

'Ah well. Plan B,' said the Pirate Captain with a disappointed shrug. He whipped his cutlass out from under his lab coat and jabbed it in the Bishop's ribs. 'I'm not really a scientist—I'm the Pirate Captain! Tell me what you've done with Erasmus!'

The Bishop didn't miss a beat. 'Why! Look over there! Is that a treasure chest?' he said.

Even though he knew better, the Pirate Captain looked over to where the Bishop was pointing. The villain took this opportunity to bolt from the lecture room. 'I just can't help myself,' thought the Pirate Captain irritably. 'Damn my piratical nature!'

He leapt to his feet, pulled off the cumbersome lab coat, and, seeing the stricken look on Darwin's face, gave the scientist a reassuring thumbs-up to show he had it all under control. Then the Pirate Captain chased as fast as he could after the despicable cleric, pausing only briefly to give his card to a striking blonde sitting in the second row.

Darwin, having little option but to hope the Pirate Captain knew what he was doing, went on hamming it up as he pretended to be desperately trying to make a wrestling tag with Mister Bobo. After a great deal of gurning and grunting he slapped the monkey's hand, and Mister Bobo leapt into centre stage and swung a folding metal chair at the head of the Holy Ghost, who promptly collapsed in a heap. Darwin held up Mister Bobo's hand triumphantly.

'Hooray for science!' he shouted. 'Tell your friends! Tell your family! And don't forget that Mister Bobo merchandise can be purchased from the museum shop!'

And with that, the audience were on their feet, giving Darwin a spectacular thunderous ovation.

The Pirate Captain skidded to a halt in the museum's cavernous main hall, realised he had lost sight of the fleeing Bishop, and said a terrible salty pirate oath. It occurred to him that the Bishop might be hiding inside the gigantic armadillo shell that was one of the Pirate Captain's favourite exhibits, but before he could check it out he was alerted by a scuffling sound from the balcony above, and so he began to charge up the marble staircase, four steps at a time, only to find an enormous slice of California redwood* rolling straight towards him. A full twenty feet in diameter, the redwood came within a whisker of crushing the Pirate Captain flat, but he just managed to dive out of the way with an athletic leap. The monstrous redwood still knocked off his pirate hat though.

---

*The California redwood is the biggest and most majestic tree in the world. Some of them can grow as high as 367 feet (13 London buses) and as broad as 22 feet in diameter (⅘ of a London bus). Their flowers are cones and they can live for over 2,000 years.

'That's my favourite hat, Bishop! You're not doing yourself any favours!'

The Pirate Captain bounded to the top of the stairs and saw the Bishop disappearing into the Hall of Fossils. Waving his cutlass and roaring, for effect more than anything, he careered inside, and almost found himself smashed in the face by a trilobite. The Bishop had a whole armful of trilobites and was flinging them at the Pirate Captain like prehistoric discuses. The Captain did his best to bat them away with his cutlass.

'Stop throwing trilobites at me!' shouted the Pirate Captain, because it was the only thing he could think of to say, given the situation. Luckily for the Pirate Captain they were not having their climactic fight in Prague Natural History Museum, which is full of trilobites and not much else, and the Bishop quickly exhausted his supply of fossils. He dashed into the adjoining room, and the Pirate Captain followed at full tilt, even though it contained the museum's collection of stuffed birds, which the Pirate Captain had always found especially creepy.

The Bishop swung a dodo at the advancing pirate, sending his cutlass flying. In return the Pirate Captain picked up an albatross and flung it squarely at the Bishop.

'Ooof!' said the Bishop, his mouth full of albatross wing. He clambered onto a balustrade and leapt from the balcony. For a moment the Pirate Captain thought the Bishop had decided to end it all, but then he realised that the wily cleric had landed on the skull of the enormous brontosaurus that was the museum's centrepiece, and was now sprinting down its bony neck to safety. The Pirate Captain jumped over the balcony himself and decided to slide down the skeleton's neck like it was a banister on the pirate boat, a decision he pretty quickly regretted. It took a moment for him to get his breath back and for his eyes to stop watering, by which time the Bishop had fled into the Mineral Room. The room's curator was surprised to see anybody coming into the Mineral Room, arguably the most boring room in the whole museum, let alone the Bishop of Oxford hotly pursued by an angry-looking pirate.

The Bishop smashed open a display case, sending a cloud of dust into the air, and flung a hefty rock at the Pirate Captain. The Pirate Captain squinted—it looked like a piece of iron as it hurtled towards his luxuriant beard. Moving lightning fast the Pirate Captain scanned the display in front of him, found a big chunk of nickel, and hurled it back towards the Bishop. The nickel hit the iron and knocked it into a thousand splinters.

'Ha!' cried the Pirate Captain. 'Nickel! Atomic weight 58.69—beats your iron, atomic weight 55.85. In your face, Bishop!'

'So let's see you deal with this!' shouted the Bishop, hefting a lump of ruthenium at the pirate.

'Ruthenium! Atomic weight 101.07! Goodness me!' cried the Pirate Captain, though perhaps in slightly saltier terms than that. He barely found a slab of osmium—atomic weight 190.2—in time.

Several elements later they were still deadlocked, and fast running out of periodic table.*

'Give up, Bishop!' said the Pirate Captain, a nugget of selenium whizzing past his ear.

'Oh, give up yourself!' shouted the Bishop, unimaginatively.

The Pirate Captain was momentarily put off when he picked up a lump of what he took to be gold, before realising it was actually iron pyrite—fool's gold, the dreaded nemesis of pirates everywhere—and his pause gave the Bishop an opportunity to escape the Mineral Room and head into the Hall of Mammals. The Pirate Captain charged after him relentlessly, but the Bishop had managed to snap the tusk off a shabby-looking walrus, and as the two men grappled he slowly inched his makeshift weapon towards the Pirate Captain's neck. The Bishop was unexpectedly strong.

'Do you work out?' asked the Pirate Captain through gritted teeth.

'A little,' said the Bishop, his face turning red. 'And yourself?'

'When I have the chance.'

'What do you bench-press?' hissed the Bishop.

'Around a hundred and ten pounds. How about you?'

---

*Mendeleyev is widely credited as being the first person to produce a 'periodic table of the elements' in 1869, but that, you'll notice, is a full thirty years after these events are supposed to be taking place. I leave readers to draw their own conclusions.

'Oh . . . a hundred and twenty . . . hundred and twenty-five . . . or thereabouts.'

'Damn.'

The trouble, reflected the Pirate Captain, was that the pirate boat's gym was covered in mirrors, so whenever he worked out he would glimpse himself pulling a ridiculously strained face, which just made him laugh and not be able to take it all that seriously. As a result he had failed to keep up with the weights regime that had been set out for him by the pirate who was a jock. But he was paying for it now. The Pirate Captain genuinely thought he was done for. The tusk pressed against his throat, cutting off his pirate breath, and as consciousness began to slip away the Pirate Captain felt like he was starting to hallucinate—it seemed as if the very exhibits behind the Bishop were writhing and coming alive! Then he realised that the exhibit behind the Bishop really *was* moving. A hairy arm reached out, there was the distinct sound of monkey fist smashing into bishop skull, and the Bishop of Oxford collapsed in a daze. The walrus tusk clattered to the floor, and the Pirate Captain looked up to see that what he had taken to be part of the stuffed chimpanzee display was actually Mister Bobo!

'Thanks for that, Mister Bobo,' said the Pirate Captain breathlessly, shaking him by the hand.

AAARGH! ME BEAUTIES! said Mister Bobo with his cards, laughing a monkey laugh.

Twelve

SWINGING FROM
THE YARDARM!

Darwin helped the Pirate Captain to his feet, and gave him back his hat.

'It's a good job I cut that question and answer session short,' he said. 'Looks like me and Mister Bobo only just got here in time.'

'No need,' said the Pirate Captain, gingerly rubbing his neck. 'I had the fiend just where I wanted him.'

'You'd started to turn blue.'

'Aaarrr. It's an old pirate trick,' said the Pirate Captain defensively. 'Not something lubbers would understand. But enough about me—how did the lecture go?'

'It was fantastic!' said Darwin with a big grin. 'I got five phone numbers from pretty girls! Five!' He waved some scraps of perfumed paper at the Pirate Captain. 'They couldn't get enough of Mister Bobo! And you were right, when he smashed that chair over the Holy Ghost's head, they almost jumped out of their seats! I'm sure they'll go home and tell everyone how shocking it all was, and how science is in the infernal pocket of Lucifer, but secretly they loved it. I've been invited to do a tour of the American universities! And Mister Bobo is going to appear on the cover of *Nature*.'

Mister Bobo gave a sheepish shrug, but you could tell he was pleased.

'Look, shall we grab a coffee?' asked Darwin. 'My shout. I've got to tell you all about the bit when I thought Scurvy Jake was actually going to sit on my head!'

'I rather think we should find out what this wretch has done with your missing brother first,' said the Pirate Captain, giving the Bishop a quick kick in the gut.

'Erasmus!' Darwin slapped his uncommonly large forehead with his palm. 'In all the excitement I'd clean forgot!'

The young scientist knelt down and shook the dazed Bishop by his bushy sideburns. 'Where is he? What have you done with my brother, you brute? I'll cut your pretty face!'

'No! Not the face!' cried the Bishop, holding up his hands to protect his beautiful skin. 'He's tied to a big cog inside Big Ben! But you're much too late—as soon as Big

Ben chimes midnight, he'll get another cog right in the chops!'

The unlikely trio hurried down to Parliament Square.

'Look! Only twenty minutes to go! How are we ever going to reach them in time?!' wailed Darwin.

'Aaarrr,' said the Pirate Captain, because he couldn't think of anything more helpful to say.

Darwin tried to look resolute. 'Climbing! It's the only way. One of us will have to climb up there!'

Big Ben loomed forbiddingly out of the fog. The Pirate Captain craned his neck, and felt a bit ill just looking up at the towering clock.

'Oh, well,' he shrugged. 'I'm afraid us pirates are notoriously rubbish at climbing up tall buildings. It's like that old shanty says . . . if a-climbing you need to go, leave those pirates down below, they're no good at it yo ho ho . . .'

It sounded to Darwin suspiciously like the Pirate Captain was making this shanty up as he went along.

'What about monkeys? They're always climbing up tall buildings! How about it Mister Bobo?' said the Pirate Captain, giving him an encouraging slap on his hairy back.

Mister Bobo chose his flash cards carefully.

| NO | F*!$%NG | WAY | signed the monkey.

'Well, Charles. It *is* your brother.'

Darwin squinted at the distant clock face and shivered.

'Ah . . . you know, me and Erasmus were never that close. He was a very solitary child. Not much of a brother at all.'

But Mister Bobo was holding up his cards again.

| WHAT | ABOUT | FITZROY | AND | HIS | AIRSHIP? | he

spelt out.

'Ah-ha!' cried the Pirate Captain. 'The little *pan-pongidae* fellow has it! We could steal the airship, pop it with my cutlass, and fashion a big rope from all the silk!'

'Or we could float up there in the airship. Because it's an airship.'

'Yes. Yes, we could do that instead. Either way's good. I'm not bothered.'

They hailed an olden-days taxi—which back in those topsy-turvy times used horses instead of electricity—and hurried back to South Kensington as fast as they could. Sprinting into the Natural History Museum, the Pirate Captain quickly grabbed his men, who he found in the gift shop buying dinosaur masks and roaring at each other.*

---

*To this day one of the best things you can buy in the Natural History Museum gift shop is a lenticular dinosaur ruler. When you waggle it back and forth, the dinosaurs appear to attack each other in an exciting fashion.

'Raagh!' roared a pirate. 'I'm a triceratops!'

'Grraagh! I'm a brontosaurus!'

It was like the usual pirate roaring, but even better. They all stopped and paid attention when the Pirate Captain burst in.

'Stop mucking about, pirates!' he shouted. 'We've got a bit of traditional pirate boarding to do!'

The pirates all flung off their scientist disguises, but several of them kept on their dinosaur masks because they figured it made them look even more fearsome than they already were. Into the gentlemen's club they charged.

'Dino-pirates!' cried a scientist, dropping his pipe in surprise. 'It's my worst nightmare!'

The Pirate Captain waved his pirate cutlass at FitzRoy and Glaisher, the airship scientist, who were sitting in a corner arguing over what the best bit about being a meteorologist was.

'It's the clouds,' FitzRoy was saying. 'Clouds are easily the best bit about meteorology.'

'Nonsense!' said Glaisher. 'It's the barometers.'

'We're boarding your airship!' bellowed the Pirate Captain. 'Prepare to be overrun! By pirates!'

FitzRoy and his friend reluctantly took the pirates round the back of the museum, to where the airship was parked. Its enormous gasbag billowed in the wind, attached by a series of sturdy ropes to a luxurious-looking gondola. The pirates all clambered aboard.

'I think this may be a first. We're taking pirating into a whole new era. They'll probably put us on stamps,' whispered the Pirate Captain to the pirate dressed in green.

'How does it float?' asked Darwin, turning to FitzRoy and Glaisher and pulling a face to show how sorry he was to be responsible for the pirates stealing their beloved airship.

'Initially we used helium as the lifting agent,' replied FitzRoy with a grimace. 'But it turned out to have a terrible and dangerous flaw.'

'Which was?'

'The pilots were always so busy larking about with the gas cylinders, making their voices go all squeaky, that they kept on smashing into trees and buildings.* So now I've switched to hydrogen. I can't see any sort of dangerous flaw when it comes to good old reliable hydrogen,' said the young captain, moving several boxes of fireworks out of the way so that he could get to the steering wheel.

'It's certainly impressive. You can tell no expense has been spared. I like what you've done with that roaring log fire next to those spare cylinders of hydrogen in the lounge,' said the Pirate Captain politely as they wandered about the gondola.

---

*Much like bananas, supplies of helium may also run out within the next twenty years. Helium is not just used in party balloons, it is also important for the manufacture of superconductors.

FitzRoy, busy throwing out ballast and letting loose the anchor rope, though annoyed to find himself being hijacked by pirates for the second time in the space of one adventure, still appreciated their compliments nonetheless.

'Be sure to check out the splendid smokers' gallery,' he said. 'You'll find it affords tremendous views of the billowing bags of hydrogen gas. And help yourself to the chops which are cooking on the airship's flaming barbecue.'

After some chops, the pirates all helped to shovel coal into the blazing furnace that powered the airship's engines.

'It's a lot quicker than a boat,' said the pirate in green appreciatively, once they were airborne.

'And that scientist is right. You *can* see down ladies' tops. Look!' exclaimed the albino pirate excitedly.

'I think I like this better than sailing. You don't get wet, and I haven't been sick once,' said the pirate who chain-smoked, lighting his cigarette and tossing away the match.

'It does have its drawbacks, mind,' cautioned FitzRoy. The albino pirate was just about to ask what sort of drawbacks there could possibly be when a low-flying crow smacked right into his face. FitzRoy sighed and shook his head sadly.

Above the ever-present fog they could see the dim lights of the city stretching out in all directions. The dirigible bobbed across central London at quite a rate, and soon they had Big Ben in sight. The Pirate Captain did a pirate gob on one of the tourists below, and was pleased to see his aim was still good.

'Heavens to Betsy!' cried Darwin. 'We've only got three minutes! We haven't time to try to find purchase on the roof. One of us will have to jump across!'

There was the unmistakable sound of several pirates staring at their fingernails.

'Honestly!' bellowed the Pirate Captain, very disappointed at his lads. 'I've been attacked by jellyfish with more backbone than you lot! Well, then. If none of you lubbers will volunteer, we'll just have to settle this the old pirate way.'

The crew looked deathly serious—the Pirate Captain could mean only one thing!

A few moments later the albino pirate took a deep breath, counted to three, and held out his clenched fist. He tried to look apologetic, but a big grin spread all across his face.

'Sorry, Captain. Pirate stone blunts your pirate scissors.'

'Whatever,' said the Pirate Captain tetchily, thinking for a moment about trying to pretend that the two fingers he was holding up were actually supposed to represent a narrow piece of paper rather than a pair of scissors. But ancient pirate tradition was ancient pirate tradition, and there was no use arguing with it. He bent down to make sure his bootlaces were done up, checked he had as big a run-up as possible, let out a mighty roar, and leapt the gap between the airship and Big Ben.

The Pirate Captain had been expecting to smash right through the gigantic glass clock face, thereby making one of his famously dramatic entrances, but he just slapped against it with a sound like a side of beef hitting a chopping board, and slowly began to slide down in a daze. Luckily the Pirate Captain had the presence of mind to grab at the huge cast-iron minute hand, and there he hung, his coattails flapping. He took a deep breath to relax himself, but the buffeting winds were doing nothing to calm his nerves and even though he didn't mean to, he glanced down. The people on the streets below looked just like ants, thought the Pirate Captain, but not regular ants, more like some kind of sinister super-ants that wore clothes and hats and carried newspapers instead of bits of leaf. Noticing the worried looks on his crew's faces as they leant anxiously out of the airship's gondola, he felt like he ought to make some sort of wisecrack in an effort to look hard-boiled and nonchalant, possibly involving a play on words with 'time', something like: 'I'm not having the TIME of my life!' But he didn't, he just grimaced a bit instead. With an effort he managed to twist himself about, and give one of the glass panels in the clock face a big kick. To the Pirate Captain's relief the panel shattered with the first blow, and after some grunting and sucking in of his gut, he was able to clamber inside.

The Pirate Captain rushed over to help Jennifer first, because she was the prettiest. He hefted the top off the big glass tube and helped her climb out. Jennifer flung her arms round his sturdy shoulders.

'Thanks! I thought I was going to end up as a bar of soap for sure! My name is Jennifer.'

'And I'm the Pirate Captain. It's a pleasure to meet you.'

'Likewise.'

'I have my own pirate boat, you know.'

'Really?'

'It has twelve cannons.'

'Goodness! That's a lot of cannons. Your beard is fantastic, by the way.'

'That's nice of you to say so. You yourself have a lovely face.'

'Oh! You're sweet.'

'Us pirates aren't just the weather-beaten rogues we're portrayed as. We have a soft side too. Also, my boat has silk sheets.'

There was a sudden sickening crunch of metal against bone, and an alarmed yelp. The Pirate Captain pulled a guilty face and slapped his forgetful forehead. He rushed over to the gigantic cog and dragged Erasmus Darwin from between its monstrous teeth.

'Sorry about that,' said the Pirate Captain with an apologetic grin. 'I'd forget my own head if it wasn't nailed down.'

'Oh! My arm!' wailed Erasmus.

'Aaarrr. Let's not get too precious about an arm,' said the Captain. 'Some of my crew don't even have legs! Just little wooden pegs. I swear, half of them are more like chairs than pirates!'*

The Pirate Captain began to untie the ropes attaching the pirate with a scarf to the huge cog.

'I wish you wouldn't get yourself into trouble like this,' he scolded his trusty number two. But he meant it in an affectionate manner. You could tell this because when the Pirate Captain scolded somebody in a manner that wasn't affectionate they tended to end up with a cutlass in their belly. 'You're definitely the best one out of my whole crew. You're worth ten of any of the rest of them'—the Pirate Captain paused and fought back a grin—'because you have so many gold teeth!'

The pirate with a scarf laughed. The Pirate Captain always made that exact same joke, but they both knew

---

*Loss of limbs was an occupational hazard for pirates. As a result most ships offered a degree of compensation for pirates injured in battle. Loss of an eye would net you 100 pieces of eight, loss of a right arm 600 pieces of eight, and loss of a left leg 400 pieces of eight.

that he really would be sorry to see anything happen to his able second in command. For a start, without help from the scarf-wearing pirate, the Pirate Captain probably wouldn't have remembered where they had left the boat. And even though the pirate with a scarf knew that he really should be disappointed by the looks Jennifer was now giving his debonair captain, for some reason he mostly just felt relieved. When it came down to it, he was much more comfortable thinking about scarves and pirating than he was thinking about ladies.

The Pirate Captain turned to give Darwin, FitzRoy, and the rest of the pirates bobbing about in the dirigible a wave through the shattered bit of clock face to show them that everything was fine, and in the process almost tripped over the pirate with an accordion, who was sprawled across the floor.

'What's up with *this* swab?' asked the Pirate Captain, nudging him with the toe of his shiny pirate boot.

'He died of scurvy, sir,' said the pirate with a scarf.

'Aaaarrr. I hope that's proved a useful lesson to you. Ham is all well and good, but make sure you get your vitamins! Scurvy is no laughing matter,' said the Pirate Captain. 'Except in those rare instances when a fellow's head swells up like a gigantic lemon,' he added as an afterthought. 'Which I grant can bring a smile even to my salty old face.'

Thirteen

TO THE
PIRATE COAST!

'. . . seven . . . eight . . . nine. Nine hams. Nine juicy hams.'

The Pirate Captain made a note on his clipboard. 'Well, that's just about everything.'

The pirates were back in Littlehampton Docks, and they had just finished loading up the pirate boat with fresh supplies of meat and grog. The only thing that remained to be wheeled on board was the pirate with an accordion, whom the other pirates had decided to have stuffed and nickel-plated, because they thought it was what he would have wanted, and besides which the pirate boat could never have too many lucky mascots. Jennifer, whom the Pirate Captain had made an honorary pirate, reckoned it was a bit on the creepy side, but pirates were a superstitious bunch.*

Darwin, Erasmus, and Mister Bobo had come down to wave them off. Darwin was almost unrecognisable from the callow youth the Pirate Captain had first met on this adventure—he had started to grow a little beard, his clothes were of the best Savile Row cut, and he had his arms round two vivacious-looking brunettes.

'Good luck then, Charles. I hope all the science goes well,' said the Pirate Captain, shaking him warmly by the hand.

'I think I'm really getting the hang of it,' said Darwin eagerly. 'I've got a lot more ideas to keep the audience on their toes. I'm going to fit a soundproofed box in the corner of my lecture theatres where I'll invite scientists too frightened to hear the shocking conclusion to my nightmarish theories to sit out the rest of the talk. And I'm offering life insurance policies to everybody in case my terrifying ideas scare them to death. I'm trying to work out a way to make all the seats vibrate. I'm calling it "Evolvovision". Me and Mister Bobo are going to be the smash-hit of Victorian science—and I owe it all to you and your pirates, Pirate Captain!'

'Aaarrrr! Don't mention it! It's been a pleasure,' said the Pirate Captain. 'I have to say, when I first saw you, I

---

*There are several seafaring superstitions. It is widely believed that redheads bring bad luck to a ship, though this can be averted if you speak to the redhead before they speak to you. Flat-footed people are also considered best avoided, as is dark-coloured luggage.

thought—there's a man whose face isn't really big enough for the size of his head. But you've proved me wrong. Oh, and by the way . . .'

The Pirate Captain paused.

'Indian, North Pacific, South Pacific, Antarctic, Arctic, North Atlantic, South Atlantic. I'm not a complete idiot, you know.'

The pirate boat slowly pulled out of the shabby dock, and all the pirates waved the steadily shrinking trio goodbye. The Pirate Captain smiled. There were good bits about the land, he reflected, like the shops and the way it didn't wobble about all the time, but he'd missed the ocean. The Pirate Captain actually became quite lost in his thoughts about how much he liked the crashing waves and seaweed and being a pirate and that, until an indignant cough jolted him back to the moment.

'And what do you propose to do with me?' said the Bishop of Oxford, who had been lashed to the boat's mast.

'We'll find an uninhabited island someplace,' said the Pirate Captain, 'and then we'll maroon you. It's the pirate way.'

'I don't much like the sound of that.'

'Oh, it's not so bad. For some reason Pirate Law says you're allowed to take a few records. And the odd book. I think it's eight of each.'

'Can I take the Bible?'

'Oh, you get that anyway. And the complete works of Shakespeare. But the rest is up to you. Don't be clever and choose *Robinson Crusoe*—everybody does that.'

The Pirate Captain turned back to watch Littlehampton's amusement arcade fade into the distance.

'That went pretty well, don't you think, number two?' he said to the pirate with a scarf.

'Yes, Captain. Though maybe our next adventure should be a little less episodic? And not be so confusing at times?' said the pirate with a scarf, leaning on the boat's safety railings and enjoying the spray of the sea on his face.

'Aaargh. You're right. And towards the last half of this adventure, I don't know if you noticed, but we stopped having half as many feasts. That was a pity.'

'And we didn't really end up with much treasure,' said the albino pirate sadly. 'Which is usually the best bit about our adventures.'

'Oh, I didn't come away completely empty-handed,' said the Pirate Captain with a grin. He rummaged about in the silky folds of his beard, where, amongst the ribbons and the luxuriant hair, something shiny seemed to be lodged. The Captain eventually prised it free. He held up a large nugget of metal. It gleamed white in the evening sun, and the pirate with a scarf whistled in admiration.

'Ruthenium!' said the albino pirate.

'Aaargh. That it is. Atomic number forty-four. Most valuable metal in the world.* Better than gold—and you know how highly I rate gold, so that's saying something.'

All the pirate crew cheered their captain, and then they went downstairs to do some shantying.

And with that, the pirate boat sailed about for a bit.

---

*Ruthenium is one of the ultra-rare 'Platinum Group metals'. It has a melting point of 2310°C and a boiling point of 3900°C, 44 protons, 44 electrons, and 57 neutrons.

COMPREHENSION EXERCISE
Answer all questions to the best of your abilities

1. What do you think the themes of this book were? Several commentators have described the main theme as 'pirates'. Another theme might be said to be 'ham'. Would you agree?

2. Which do you think is more important to the Pirate Captain—ham, or his luxurious beard? If you had to choose which was more important to you, which one do you think you would pick?

3. On *The Late Show,* one of the critics, who has a face that looks like it's made of mallow, said to Germaine Greer, 'I wish there were more of Black Bellamy in *The Pirates! In an Adventure with Scientists,* he was the best character ever.' Would you agree with this assessment?

4. Who do you think should play the Pirate Captain if they were ever to make a movie of this book?

5. Do you think the section in Chapter Five when the Pirate Captain forces several pirates to walk the plank is included to show that life at sea had a harsh edge to it? Or do you think the author has some other motives?

6. Choose the letter that best represents your feelings: 'Upon completion of *The Pirates! In an Adventure with Scientists,* I would describe my mood as _____

(A) angry   (B) restless   (C) excitable
(D) sleepy   (E) afraid

7. Scientifically speaking, who do you think the tallest pirate in the world is?

THANK YOU

WORDS TO KNOW

lubber   pirate   starboard

ham   sloop   galley

ACKNOWLEDGEMENTS

First, to Richard Murkin, because this book is the product of us knocking about for the last ten years. Thanks also to Helen Garnons-Williams for her ace editing, Claire Paterson for her ace agenting, and Caitlin Moran for actually sending it to Claire in the first place. I should mention that David Cordingly's *Life Among the Pirates* and Bodenstandig 2000's *Maxi German Rave Blast Hits 3* both came in very useful when I was writing this.

Plus (for a load of different reasons) my mum, Sam Brown, Chloe Brown, Rob Adey, Nicola Hughes, Dr. Jack Button, Danny Garlick, Sherhan Lingham, and Rebecca Andrews. And Ruth.